YOUNG FAMILY'S AUTUMN BLESSINGS

By Lola

ISBN-10: 0-9981297-1-2
ISBN-13: 978-0-9981297-1-6

DEDICATION

To my husband, Larry, who has taken on the difficult task of being my assistant. I also dedicate this book to a long list of family and friends with love! I appreciate the loving encouragement, patience and support that I've received from them.

My beautiful daughters and grandchildren are my love and inspiration!

A Special Thanks To:

Mary W. for being my longtime extended family and prayer partner!

Sandra K. for her role in helping me bravely follow my heart. She has provided me with renewed strength to fulfill my life's journey!

Shannon C. for being there with encouraging words and loving support throughout this book-writing journey!

Tammy G. for being my longtime friend and my Dream Team Partner!

PREFACE

This book is fiction. It's second in 'The Young Family' series. This fiction story picks up where my first book, 'Love Grows in Omaha', ends. The fictional characters are the Young family and their extended family members. It's a love story about the adventures shared by these families in a make-believe city, Omaha, as they celebrate the holidays and blessings associated with the autumn season.

TABLE OF CONTENT

CHAPTER ONE
GOODBYE, SUMMER!

When Gary Young returned home from his summer vacation in July, he decided to take a sabbatical by spending more time at his lake house. He temporarily took up residence there to enjoy the benefits of his little paradise. Moving out of his big house permanently is not an option for him. He believes that he won't be happy living alone. He's not ready to give up the beautiful home and garden that is filled with treasured memories.

He loves being in the great outdoors! In September, the weather is still perfect for fishing and boating. Relaxing while watching a sunrise and/or a sunset has a way of reenergizing him. He frequently invites his beloved family and friends out for get-togethers. They enjoy picnics by the lake or in the garden gazebo. There's always a great deal of laughter when they go boating and fishing.

He's taking time to rest and adjust to this new stage of his life. His son, Jonny, became engaged to Mandy last month. They've decided to plan their wedding for spring of next year. Mandy excitedly shares little tidbits about her dream wedding with her Mom, Katherine. Gary cares very much for Katherine and maintains a close relationship as friends. Sadie spends most of her time now with her family and Charlie. Gary has kept in close touch with everyone via his cell phone and video chatting on his laptop.

Autumn is in the air and the aroma is cleaner as well as crisper. Breathing in this fresh air is invigorating. The days and nights are getting colder.

Autumn leaves on the trees by the lake are especially a bright array of beautiful brown, orange, amber and gold colors.

Gary is happy resting at the lake house but plans to move back to his house in early October. First, he intends to winterize the lake house, yard and boat. It isn't hard work but proves to be time consuming. The winters in Omaha can be brutal with blizzards, snow and ice. Traveling on the country roads between the lake house and home can be dangerous.

It's the last weekend in September. Friday night, an unexpected thunderstorm with high winds is blowing through the lakeside community. Gary sleeps through the storm in the den where the fireplace is keeping him warm. Saturday morning, Gary wakes up and discovers a power outage as well as several broken tree branches on the ground.

He feels fortunate to have a gas stove in his kitchen. He prepares his morning coffee and breakfast. While he's eating breakfast, he receives a call on his cell phone. He answers it with a cheerful hello because he hears that the caller is Jonny.

"Hello, Son! How are you doing?"

"Hello, Dad, I'm just fine. I'm calling to see how you're doing. I just heard about the thunderstorm that was in your area last night."

"I managed to sleep through the storm. I'm up, drinking coffee and almost finished eating my breakfast. The power is out in this area. I haven't been outside to investigate, yet. When I looked out the kitchen window, I noticed several broken tree branches on the ground."

"I'm free today. I would like to drive out to the lake house to visit with you. I can give you a hand cleaning up the yard. I had a busy week at work. It'll do me a world of good to get out and take in a little outdoor activity as well as a breath of fresh air.'

"Sure, Son, A visit with you today will be greatly appreciated. It's not necessary for you to help me clean up the yard. But if you want to, your help will get the job done a lot faster."

"I'll drive out to see you soon, Dad. I'm going to take a few minutes to change into my working outdoors clothes." They both chuckle.

"Okay, sounds great. By the way, the power has just been restored. See you soon, Jon."

Gary cleans up the kitchen and pours another mug of coffee. He grabs his jacket and puts on his hat while heading out the back door. He stops and looks around to see what kind of tools he will need from the shed. His work gloves and boots are on a shelf close to the items he will need to clean up the yard.

He thinks to himself, "*It will be exciting to relive some of the memories of working with Jonny here when he was younger. I can remember when we used to work together to winterize the house, boat, and garden. Now that he's running the businesses, he'll be too busy or too tired to help me with all of that this year. It'll be okay, but I do miss those fun times.*"

He locates and removes the rake, yard-size trash bags, wheelbarrow and a saw from the shed. He pushes the wheelbarrow around in the backyard and in the front yard to pick up small branches. There a few small branches and twigs in the garden along with dead flowers that will need to be cleaned up, too.

He spies his boat secured along his dock and makes a mental note. *"I need to winterize the boat and store it at the Community Boat House."*

Continues to think, *"I'll postpone the yard work for now. I'm sure we won't take the boat out again this year. I'll give Jon a call and let him know where I'll be. If he arrives and doesn't see me here, he might worry."*

He takes his cell phone out of his pocket to call Jonny but stops and returns it. He hears Jonny's car pulling into the driveway. In a heartbeat, Jonny walks around the corner of the lake house. He's excited to see his Dad today. They hurriedly walk toward each other and embrace with big smiles.

"Jon, I was just getting ready to give you a call. So, glad that you made it safely. It's so good to spend this time with you here. Would you like a mug of coffee? We can go in and visit by the fireplace to warm up again."

"That sounds great, Dad."

They go into the house and head for the kitchen. Gary warms up his coffee by adding more from the coffee pot. Jonny grabs a mug off the hook under the counter. He fills his mug with the fresh hot coffee.

"Jon, would you like something to eat? How about a Danish? That will taste good with the coffee."

"Sounds great, I'll get the plates for us out of the cabinet."

Gary places an apple Danish on each of their plates. They both head toward the den to visit by the fireplace. They place their mugs and plates on side tables by the two overstuffed chairs.

Just like old times, Jonny stirs the embers while Gary places two more logs on the fire. The pleasant aroma of cedar fills the room. They smile at each other as they listen to the popping and crackling sounds.

They make themselves comfortable in their chairs while they drink their coffee. The warmth, sounds and aroma of the fireplace is very comforting, like a gentle bear hug.

Father and Son chatter away about anything and everything. It's been a long time since the two of them sat down together and shared old family memories. They chat about business and how Mandy is handling the job as Assistant. The autumn weather and the beautiful changes that surround the lake house is discussed. Clearly, they agree that the summer days flew by in a flash. With that said, they seriously talk about the work that needs to be done to winterize the house, garden and boat. Finally, they talk about what needs to be done to clean up after last night's storm.

Jonny says, "Dad, I noticed when I arrived, you were busy picking up small branches and twigs. I also noticed some larger branches on the ground. Would you like to go work outside now? The two of us working together can get the job done faster. I'm willing to help in any way that I can. I'm ready to get started whenever you are."

They exchange a quick father and son hug with big smiles. First, they walk back to the kitchen and refill their mugs with hot coffee to take with them outside. Jonny finds his work gloves and work boots from last year in the storage shed. He quickly changes and follows his Dad over to the wheelbarrow. When the smaller twigs and branches are collected, they fill the trash bags. Together, they gather up the larger branches and use a saw to cut them in smaller pieces. Johnny is busy tying them up in small bundles when he hears his cell phone chime.

He answers the call right away because he knows by the ringtone that it's Mandy. He answers his phone with a cheerful greeting. "Hello, Mandy, my love! How are you?"

"Hello, Jonny, my love. I'm fine and you? Do you have plans for today?"

"I'm out at the lake house right now. There was a thunderstorm out here last night. I'm helping my Dad clean up the yard. I'll be busy helping him with tree limbs and raking up the leaves. It's a beautiful day here with the sun shining but it's chilly. We'll need to work fast before the sun sets and the temperature drops. What are you up to, today, sweetheart?"

"I finished cleaning my apartment and taking care of the usual Saturday morning confusion. I'm free to go out and about. My reason for calling is to ask you out for lunch? Since you are busy helping your Dad at the lake house, I'll ask you if you would like my help there, too? I used to help my Mom and Dad with the yard work. I'm perfectly capable and willing to help you rake the leaves and work in the garden."

"Mandy, that is an absolutely wonderful idea. Thank you for offering. My Dad will surely thank you, too. He's planning to winterize the house, garden and boat this weekend. The clean up after the storm sets back his schedule. He has plans to move back to the bigger house next week."

"Okay, I'll drive out there soon while there's still daylight. It's kind of late for a lunch date anyway but is there anything I can bring out there for all of us to eat for a late lunch together?"

"Why don't you go ahead and drive out and then we can check with Dad and see what is available in the kitchen? This sounds like a fun way for us to enjoy the Autumn weather. You'll love seeing the beautiful the autumn leaves and breathing in the crisp clean air."

"Sounds like a good plan. I'll arrive there shortly. I love you, Jonny!"

"I love you, Mandy. See you soon!"

Jonny finds his Dad searching in the shed for more string to tie up the branches.

"Mandy called to invite me on a lunch date. She didn't know that I was here helping you clean up after the storm. She is coming out to help."

Gary is grateful, of course, because the work is very time consuming. Having another pair of helping hands will get the job done even faster.

Jonny asks, "Do you have any food in the house that the three of us can use for a lunch break?"

"I have a variety of soups to choose from. There's meat and cheese from the local deli in the refrigerator. I've got a loaf of sandwich bread. Would you like potato chips or corn chips? This would be the perfect time to open the bottle of Apple Cider.

Warm Apple Cider always tastes great this time of year."

"That all sounds wonderful to me, Dad. Why don't we go in and build up the fire again? We can be warm and comfy when we eat our lunch?"

"Yes, that's a good idea. Do you know when she'll be here?"

"She's on her way and will arrive here soon."

CHAPTER TWO
HELLO, AUTUMN!

While waiting for Mandy to arrive, Gary places several logs on the fire in the fireplace. Once again, the aroma, the sounds and warmth fills the house. They're sure that she'll sense a level of comfort that says, "welcome home"

Jonny sets the table for three at a cozy kitchen table. They work together to prep the kitchen. They locate the food items that they need to serve a hearty lunch. Gary is delighted to put his talent to work by heating and adding spices to the Apple Cider.

They smile at each other as the aroma of apples and spices fills the air. Jonny says, "The cider smells so good and reminds me of Mom. She loved the Holidays. She baked apple and pumpkin pies with Sadie. The familiar aroma also reminds me that the holidays are right around the corner."

"I certainly agree with you, Son. Time flies by this time of year. It seems the holidays come and go quickly. We'll celebrate with new friends and family this year. I'm glad that we could spend this time together out here in the beauty of autumn colors. The time that I've spent with you today is priceless."

"I've enjoyed our time together, too. I'm happy that Mandy will be joining us soon. She's one very special lady and I look forward to her being part of our family. I still wish that Mom could be here.'"

"I feel the same way. I still miss Angela very much! We'll make the best of it. Mandy should be here any minute."

"I think I would like to eat chicken noodle soup with a sandwich. Are you up for that? We can wait until Mandy arrives and let her vote count, too. I'll slice the tomatoes and onions for our sandwiches."

"Okay, I'll clean a few lettuce leaves for our sandwiches, too. Maybe she'll want a salad instead. We still have a lot to learn about our dear Mandy." They both smile at each other in a loving and understanding way.

"One thing I know for sure, Dad, is that I love her very much! I really believe that she loves me, too!"

They hear a voice! It's Mandy at the back door. She playfully says, "Knock! Knock! Is anybody home?" They hear her giggling and start laughing.

Jonny goes to the door and they exchange a hello hug and kiss. Mandy walks toward Gary and they exchange a welcoming hug.

"I'm so happy to be here visiting with you again, Gary. Autumn is in the air. There's a stark contrast between the time I spent here in the summer and the way things appear now. Your little paradise is beautiful with the colorful autumn leaves."

Jonny says, "Let me take your jacket and hat. I'll hang them up for you in the closet."

Gary says, "I think the apple cider is ready to drink now. Would you two like a cup?"

They reply, "Yes, please! The cider smells delicious!"

Gary serves the warm apple cider in designer mugs. The festive mugs brighten up the table setting.

Jonny pulls out a chair for Mandy to sit down at the table.

They discuss the kind of soup and sandwich that they want to eat for their lunch. Because they agree unanimously on the Chicken Noodle Soup, Gary prepares it in a small crockpot. It'll stay warm long enough to fill the sandwich orders. Gary sets out the bread and deli tray in the middle of the table. Johnny sets out the sliced vegetable tray.

Mandy prepares her sandwich and offers to fix one for each of the men. They tell her to just relax and that they'll join her at the table in a couple of minutes. Gary serves the soup in bowls and sets them down on the table. He takes a seat at the head of the table.

Jonny asks, "Is there anything else that you would like to eat, Dad and Mandy? How about a condiment for your sandwich? Would you like potato or corn chips?"

Both Mandy and his Dad tell him that everything is good now. Jonny sits down on a chair between his Dad and Mandy. There's a couple of minutes of silence and sighs of relief. They're at peace sitting together as a family while enjoying a hearty meal.

There's not a lot of conversation because they know that there's work to be done outside before the sun goes down and the temperature drops. There are lots of smiles and eye contact while they fill up on their soup and sandwich. When they're finished eating, Mandy takes charge and clears the table. She puts the leftover food back into the refrigerator. Gary decides to leave the soup in the crockpot on a low/warm setting for later.

Mandy thanks them for the delicious meal and cider. She comments on the fire in the fireplace as she warms her hands by it. She asks, "Are we ready to head outside to clean up the yard, now?"

Gary says, "Oh, just before you two arrived, I remembered that today would be a good day to take the boat over to Greg at the Community Boat House. Do you want to give me a hand with that chore first?"

Jonny and Mandy agreed to help in any way that they can. They ask Gary what exactly can they do to help with the boat.

Gary asks, "Jonny, do you remember the boat house on the other side of the lake? Greg has been winterizing and storing the boat there for many years now. Will you be okay with driving the boat to the other side of the lake and docking it at their pier? I'll drive over in the jeep and meet you there."

"Yes, Dad, I remember the boat house and Greg. Mandy, would you like to ride with me in the boat or would you like to ride over with Dad in the jeep?"

"It's a little chilly for a boat ride but it's so beautiful outdoors. It will be great to see the autumn scenery. Do you have a blanket that I can use to wrap up in?" She giggles and says, "I don't think my jacket will be warm enough. The spray of water from the lake that we enjoyed in the summer, won't be quite as enjoyable now."

Gary goes to the linen closet and pulls out a knitted afghan and hands it to Mandy. He hands Jonny the keys to the boat. The three of them put on their hats and jackets to keep warm. They're excited to get the job done and for the new adventure. This is the first-time Jonny will drive the boat across the lake. The first-time Mandy visits at the lake house during the Autumn season.

They head out the back door and walk down to the lake where the boat is secured to the dock. Gary inspects the inside of the boat to be sure that no personal items were left behind and hidden under benches.

Jonny helps Mandy settle in to the passenger seat. After he settles in and starts up the engine, his Dad unties the ropes. He has mixed feelings as he watches them grow smaller in the distance. He misses the summer family time fun already! He's flooded with memories as he watches his little boy that is now all grown up. He quickly dries the tears in his eyes.

He hurries to the jeep and drives around the lake to the boat house. He spies Greg and they greet each other with a smile and a friendly wave. They meet up with Jonny and Mandy at the boat by the dock. Jonny is busy tying the ropes to secure it. He carefully helps Mandy out of the boat and onto the dock. She still has the afghan wrapped around her shoulders. They're smiling and one can tell they're very much in love. The joyful look in their eyes sparkles.

Greg says, "So good to see you again, Gary and Jonny. Who is this beautiful young lady?"

Jonny introduces Mandy to Greg as his fiancé and soon-to-be bride. Greg is thrilled and extends a hand to greet her. He says, "It's a pleasure to meet you, Mandy."

Mandy says, "I'm happy to meet you, too."

Greg asks Gary, "Do you want the usual service and storage for your boat?"

Gary confidently says, "Yes, I know that you'll take good care of her during the cold weather months. I know that she'll be in good hands with you and your crew."

"Yes, we'll take good care of her Gary because you are truly a good friend. Tomorrow, I'll have one of my workers drain the fluids so they don't freeze. I see that your tarp is folded there in the back of the boat. We'll cover her up and tie down the tarp to protect her from the elements. She'll be stored under the canopy and hoisted up on a cradle out of the water. Just like we have in the past, we'll take good care of her."

"Thank you, Greg, I'll write a check for you right now to cover the cost of storage between now and late spring as well as the cost of maintenance." He writes out the check and hands it to Greg. They shake hands, smile and agree to meet again in Spring.

Gary drives the jeep with Jon and Mandy around the lake back to the house. They go inside to warm up by the fireplace and drink another mug of apple cider. They visit by the fireplace long enough to decide what to do next.

The men are almost finished with cleaning up the branches and twigs. Gary says, "I can finish bagging up the tree branches and twigs. Would you and Mandy like to start raking those beautiful leaves? We can use some of them spread over the plants in the garden. Some of the plants will survive the winter if we can cover them."

Mandy asks, "Where are the rakes, Jonny? I'll get started in the front yard. The leaves in the front are not very thick. It'll be easier for me to rake them first. Of course, they're still wet from the storm last night but we can bag them for the recycling service to pick them up."

"I have one rake here and I think we can find another in the storage shed. Let's go look. Do you have work gloves to wear? I think that there's a small pair that you can wear."

"Yes, this pair of gloves will work just fine. Thank you! Ok, we have two rakes and yard bags. Do you want to get started in the front yard now? It's really chilly out here."

"Come closer, Mandy, I'll help keep you warm. I'll wrap my arms around you real tight." He kisses her on the forehead and they exchange a very loving and passionate kiss. "Yes, we better get started with the chore of raking leaves. There are a lot of trees and leaves are falling as we stand here. They both smile and laugh as they continue to embrace.

They go to work raking the colorful wet leaves into piles and fill the yard bags. Mandy shares a few childhood memories about how she helped her Mom and Dad rake leaves in their yard. They would make a game out of it. She tells Jonny how she would run through the leaves and fall laughing on top of the pile. Of course, these leaves are too wet and too cold for that kind of fun.

Jonny carries the full bags of leaves and leans them up against the side of the house. He's not sure where his Dad places them for the pick-up service. They move around to the back of the house. They start raking the leaves that have fallen from the trees along the lake. The piles of autumn leaves are a mixture of beautiful shades of red, orange, brown and yellow colors.

CHAPTER THREE
SATURDAY NIGHT

Mandy and Jonny simultaneously laugh at the sight of the backyard swing. The bench is filled with colorful leaves. They walk over to the two-seater swing, smile and embrace. She pulls out her cell phone and takes a memento photo.

He brushes off the leaves and says, "Let's take a little break. We first declared our love for each other on this swing."

She says, "We shared our first kiss on this swing in the Spring.! Let's take a photo sitting here together."

He pulls out his phone and says, 'This photo reflects our love and autumn's beauty. It's perfect for our family photo album."

"I want a copy of this pic, please. Or smile and I will take one of my own on my phone." They cuddle in again and smile while she takes their photo with her phone.

They both take random shots of the area because the area is just a beautiful little paradise. He notices that his Dad is working in the garden. He snaps a couple of photos of him to add to their album.

They're finished with the chore of raking the leaves. They walk over to his Dad and ask, "How many piles of leaves will you need to mulch the garden plants? We will help cover the plants when you're ready and then we can put the rest in bags."

His Dad replies, "I still need to trim back the sweetheart roses before I cover the plants with leaves. I can handle that chore by myself. I appreciate your hard work and time that you spent here helping. What I can't finish doing today, I can finish tomorrow because the weather is supposed to be better."

"If you want us to help tomorrow, please give us a call. We'll be here for you. Mandy and I are feeling hungry again. Would you like to take a break and join us for dinner? We'll probably go to a local restaurant. We don't want to put you out and would be happy to treat you. You've been working hard. I bet you're too tired to cook anything for yourself."

"I really want to finish taking good care of Angela's favorite flowers before I take a break. I'm almost done here. I think you two should run along then so that you can enjoy your Saturday night together. I have leftover chicken soup that I can eat when I'm hungry. It's still warm in the crockpot and perfect for this chilly weather. I'll be fine!"

"Okay, Dad. We'll go ahead and take off then." Jonny and his Dad smile and share a goodbye hug. Mandy also reaches out to give her future father-in-law a goodbye hug. They say their Goodbyes and say, "See you later," as they walk toward the driveway,

They take time to put away the rakes and a few other items in the shed. While they stand there gazing into each other's eyes, they exchange a warm embrace and a kiss.

Jonny says, "Thank you for helping us out here today. We appreciate it very much. It's Saturday night, how about a dinner date? You can choose the restaurant."

"I'm really hungry and tired. I think we should go home from here to get cleaned up. There is an Italian Restaurant close to my apartment that we should check out. Would you like to eat Italian food tonight? It's a family restaurant but I hear the food is good. We can dress casually and really relax."

"Yes, of course, that sounds really great. You can give me a call or text me when you're ready and I will drive over and pick you up. I'll want to clean up and change my clothes before we go out, also."

He walks with her to her car. Before he walks away to his car, they exchange a passionate kiss goodbye.

She arrives at her apartment tired but excited about going out on a Saturday night. She gets ready to go out to dinner with Jonny in a flash. As he suggested, she sends him a brief text letting him know that she will be waiting for his arrival. He replies with a text that he's on his way!

He stops at a floral shop to buy her a bouquet of autumn flowers. He arrives at her apartment a short time after that with flowers in hand and rings the doorbell. She answers the door with a happily surprised smile.

As he walks in she says, "Oh, thank you so much for the beautiful flowers. You are so romantic!"

They walk over to the kitchen to place the flowers in a vase and in the center of the table. He asks, "Would you like to go out to dinner now or do you want to wait a little longer?"

"I'm hungry. If you're hungry then we should go to the restaurant now before gets too crowded and loud."

"Ok, we can leave now." He helps her with her jacket and says, "Mandy, you really look beautiful as always!" He kisses her on the back of her neck. She turns around and they exchange a loving hug and passionate kiss.

He drives them to the local Italian restaurant. She doesn't know it but he called ahead for a reservation before he went to her door. He was lucky to reserve a table for two in a quiet corner. It's a family restaurant but there is a section that is separate and decorated for couples in a candle light setting.

She's quite surprised and excited to be seated in a relaxing and romantic atmosphere. He's the perfect gentleman and stays one step ahead of her needs. He helps remove her jacket and pulls out the chair for her to sit down comfortably. They settle in with the menus that the waiter left for them on their table.

They're not sure what to order because this is their first time to dine there. He asks the waiter what he would suggest. The waiter, Don, says, "I would start you off with a glass of our best wine. If you would like an appetizer, I suggest stuffed mushrooms. The chef's special tonight is Cheese Tortellini with your choice of sauce. We have a variety of sauces to choose from. It comes with a bread basket and a salad. Would you like to order that for your meal tonight? Do you need more time to read the menus?"

Jonny and Mandy make eye contact and smile with a nod that of approval. Jonny says, "We're willing to try what you suggested."

He asks Mandy, "What kind of sauce do you want to order? I'm going to try the meat sauce."

She replies, "I prefer the alfredo sauce. It all sounds good to me. Thank you!"

Jonny places their order and in a short time, a waitress from the bar serves them a glass of wine. They're talking and holding hands when the waiter delivers the appetizer to their table. So far everything is going well. Wine and appetizer are delicious! The atmosphere is relaxing after a long day.

They wait patiently for their main course. They use the time to chat about this and that. When their food finally arrives, it is tasty but the hour is getting late. They're both feeling the exhaustion and are feeling a little sore from the yard work. Anxious to return home for a chance to relax, Jonny pays the bill and tip. He helps Mandy with her jacket and they leave the restaurant.

He drives to her apartment and she invites him in. They cuddle on the couch and talk about the day and any plans they might have for tomorrow. She's feeling very relaxed and sleepy. He says, "I'll let you get the sleep you need for tonight and I'll call you tomorrow. I love you!" He kisses her goodnight and walks toward the door to leave.

"Wait, Jonny, I love you! Drive safe! You look very tired, too! I look forward to getting your call tomorrow." They exchange a long passionate hug and several passionate goodnight kisses! Now, he doesn't want to leave and she wants him to stay.

"I really need to go, sweetheart, it's late and we both need to rest after the work we accomplished today. I'm hoping we can spend some fun time together tomorrow. Although, depending on what Dad has planned, he might need more help at the lake house. If you think about something that you want to do for fun, we can do it."

"I had fun working at the lake house and eating lunch with you and your dad. If he needs more help, I'm willing to spend the day there with you, too."

"We'll see what happens tomorrow. I'll say goodnight and leave now so that we can both get the rest that we need for tomorrow." They kiss, hug and say good night one more time before he walks out the door.

She does what she needs to do and goes to bed for a good night's sleep. Jonny arrives home to a big empty house. He's thinking of his Dad hoping that he's alright after the long hard day he put in at the lake house. *'I'll give Dad a call tomorrow to ask if he's doing okay.'* He's exhausted and sore but makes his way up the stairs and gets ready for bed. He falls asleep within a minute of resting his head on the pillow.

In the meantime, Gary finished the chore of taking care of Angela's roses. He finished winterizing the garden, set the bags of leaves at the curb for pick up and stored away outdoor patio items in the storage shed. The sunset is gorgeous but he's tired, cold and hungry so he calls it a day.

Once inside, he builds up the fire in the fireplace. He eats the leftover chicken soup with half of a cheese sandwich for supper. He takes a mug of cider into the den to relax. He enjoys the warmth of the fireplace before getting ready for bed. He puts his feet up on the ottoman and rests with his eyes closed for a few minutes. Lots of thoughts and memories are flooding his mind.

He thinks, *'I would like to finish the work I need to do here and move my personal belongings back to the big house tomorrow. There's not a lot left to do since the kids gave me a hand today.'*

He locates a tablet and pen to make a checklist of things that he'll need to do tomorrow. Number one is to be sure to turn off the water so that the pipes don't freeze. Number two, turn down the heater to about 50 degrees to help keep the house somewhat warm until we return over the holidays. *'I think Mandy will love it here when the lake freezes over. I wonder if she knows how to ice skate?! Since the outdoor work and boat is taken care of, I'll need to focus on the inside.'* Next on his list is the clean dust covers that he put in the linen closet in the spring. He will cover the furniture before he leaves the house. Oh, yes, the chimney will need to be closed but he'll call a chimney cleaning service to take care of that on Monday.

His thoughts start drifting as he becomes sleepier. He gets ready for bed and falls asleep on the couch by the fireplace. His last thoughts are of Angela, Jon, Mandy, Katherine and Sadie as well his many friends. He dreams about getting together with his loved ones again soon. Several memories from past holidays are mixed in his dreams. A flurry of ideas begins to rush in about celebrating the holidays this year with his new friends. He sleeps peacefully on this Saturday night.

CHAPTER FOUR
NO PLACE LIKE HOME

Mandy wakes up in the middle of the night chilled, sneezing and feeling congested. She goes to her medicine cabinet and takes cold medicine. She's wide awake so goes to the kitchen to make a cup of hot tea with lemon and honey. She drinks the tea in the living room while sitting on her couch. She cuddles in an afghan to warm up because she's feeling chilled-to-the-bone.

She thinks, *'Perhaps working outdoors in the chilly and wet air yesterday is catching up with me. Hopefully the tea and med will give me the relief I need to get back to sleep. I really need the rest.'* She drifts off to sleep again on the couch! She doesn't wake up again until 8:00am in the morning. Since she doesn't have any plans for the day, she decides to take another dose of cold med and goes back to her comfy bed. Before moving back to her room, she drinks a glass of orange juice for a little extra vitamin C.

She's still wrapped in the afghan from the couch as she curls up in her bed. As she falls fast asleep, she misses a call on her cell phone. The cold med makes her drowsy which helps her to sleep like a baby.

Her Mom, Katherine, is up early on a Sunday morning. She calls Mandy on her cell phone but the call goes directly to voicemail. Her Mom leaves a message – "Mandy, dear, it's Mom! I'm calling to ask you if you'd like to join me for brunch today.   Please give me a call so that we can make plans. Love, you!"

Mandy wakes up again at noon but she's still coughing, sneezing and feeling congested. The light on her phone is flashing. She checks it to see who called. She listens to the voicemail message from her Mom. Feeling disappointed, she calls her Mom and apologizes for not hearing her phone.

In a very nasal sounding voice, she says, "I wish that we could have brunch, Mom, but I really don't feel very well today. I think that I'll stay in and rest so that I'll be able to go the office tomorrow. I think that I might have a cold. I worked outdoors with Jonny and his Dad. It was chilly and wet yesterday at the lake house."

"I hope you feel better soon. If I can help in any way, please let me know. I'll let you get back to bed so that you can get your rest. I'll check back with you this evening. I love you, my dear!"

"Thanks, Mom. I love you, too! Talk later!"

Mandy dresses in her robe over a pair of warm pajamas. She goes to the kitchen and drinks another glass of orange juice. While she turns the kettle on for another cup of hot tea, she calls Jonny.

Jonny answers, "Hello, Mandy! Have you been up long? I was just thinking about calling you. I just finished eating breakfast and you're on my mind. What would you like to do today?"

She's so chilled that her teeth are chattering. She replies with a nasal tone, "Hello Jonny! I'm not up for doing anything today. I woke up in the middle of the night chilled, sneezing and very congested. I've been taking a cold med regularly and I just slept in. I'm making a cup of hot tea with lemon and honey, again. I'm doing all that I can to treat this cold. I don't want to miss work tomorrow. I'll be staying home today to get the rest that I need."

"Aw, Mandy, darling. I'm so sorry to hear that. I should check with Sadie about the availability of her famous chicken soup. I can bring some soup over to you today and hold you in my arms. I can give lots of TLC to you."

"I don't know if I'm contagious. I don't want you to get sick, too. I'll be alright if I can just feel well enough to go to work tomorrow. I'll spend the day resting and treating myself kindly. Thank you for offering to bring Sadie's soup to me. I admit that sounds good to me. Have you heard from your Dad, yet?"

"Yes, I called my Dad earlier. He rises with the sun and I wanted to know what his plans are for the day. He said that he plans to pack up his personal belonging and return to the big house for the holidays. He has a short to-do-list that he needs to complete and then he'll be heading home."

"That's great Jonny, I'm so glad that he's doing well after the work he put in yesterday. I need to go take care of myself, Jonny. I'll call you back a little later. I want to soak in a hot bath, eat my breakfast, drink the hot tea and take another dose of cold med. I'll give you another call before I snuggle back into bed for a little more rest today. My Mom called to invite me to brunch but I didn't feel up to going out. I'm sad that I missed a chance to visit with her."

"I understand how you feel. Ok, please call if there's anything that I can do to help you feel better. Rest well. I love you!"

"I love you, too, Jonny! Enjoy your Dad's return home today! Wish I could be there. I know that he will be very happy to be home again. I think the sabbatical was a very wise choice for him."

"I agree and I do look forward to seeing him back home and visiting with him daily. He's a great Dad! I feel blessed to be living here with him. Please feel better soon, Mandy. We'll make a date to visit over here with Dad again soon. I know that he'll like having the family together again."

"That sounds great. I'll say goodbye now. Take good care of you, Jonny! Hope to feel better and see you in the office tomorrow. Talk later."

"Bye my darling Mandy. Talk soon!"

She eats breakfast including a glass of orange juice, hot tea with lemon and honey. She's feeling somewhat refreshed but anxious to soak in a bubble bath. While she's running the water in the tub, her phone rings. Her phone is still on the kitchen table. She doesn't hear it ringing. It's Jonny with an update but it goes directly to voicemail. He leaves a message.

"Hi Mandy, good news, I talked to Sadie and she said she would be happy to make the chicken soup for you today. It'll take time for her to cook it. I'll bring it over this evening in time for your supper.

She relaxes and thinks to herself. *"Ah, I really needed this hot bath for my sore muscles as well as for my cold.*

She starts to drift off because of the cold med making her feel drowsy. She dresses in a new pair of clean pajamas and snuggles back into bed. She's so sleep that she forgets to pick up her phone from the kitchen.

Gary has completed his to do list to winterize the lake house. He's packed all his belongings in his jeep and is heading home. As he makes the drive through the country roads, he recalls the good time he had at the lake house. He enjoyed the outdoor experience of summer changing into autumn. He's feeling energized and looking forward to being home again. He knows that he'll have a chance to spend time at the lake house again soon. He recalls winter activities that his family enjoyed there over the years. When the lake was frozen, they enjoyed ice fishing and ice skating as a family. He's hopeful that they can do those fun activities together again this year.

He arrives home and is happy to find Jon waiting with big smiles and open arms. They exchange a quick father-son hug.

"Welcome home, Dad! We sure have missed you around here." Jon scurries out to the jeep and carries in a suitcase and a couple of grocery bags. Between the two of them, they unpack the jeep in a very short time. They sit down in the living room in their comfortable recliners. Jon fills in his Dad on Mandy's condition.

"That's too bad about Mandy getting sick. She put forth lots of effort yesterday at the lake house. I hope she feels better soon."

"I spoke with Sadie about cooking her chicken soup for Mandy. She said that she would make it at her house. I'll stop by there later. Mandy is hopefully resting now. I called and left a message that I would bring it by in time for supper. What about you, Dad? Do you have plans for dinner yet?"

"Not yet. I'm going to focus on getting unpacked and settled. After I take care of that chore, we can talk about our plans for dinner. I'm sure taking the soup over to Mandy and visiting with her will take up most of your time."

"We'll see how that works out. I'm still waiting for Mandy to return my call. She probably slept through the ringtone."

"I'm going to take my personal belongings upstairs and unpack my suitcases. Would you mind putting away a few groceries that I brought from the lake house? I will appreciate it if you would put the cold food in the refrigerator. I can take care of the dry goods later. I'm anxious to settle in. I'm really happy to be home again."

"Sure, Dad. I'll put it all away for you. I'm happy you are home and want you to settle in and relax. You've had a busy day already with the work you did to prep the lake house for the winter months. We'll visit again after you're finished upstairs. I'll let you know when I hear from Sadie about the soup. Then we can talk about dinner plans and scheduling the best time to visit with Mandy."

"Sounds great, Jon!"

"Would you like for me to carry a couple of the suitcases upstairs?"

"No, I've got it. Thanks!"

Jonny unpacks grocery bags in the kitchen while his Dad is busy unpacking suitcases and settling in. Sadie is finished cooking the chicken soup for Mandy.

She calls him on the cell phone. "Hello Jonny, the chicken soup is done for Mandy."

"Thank you so much, Sadie. I'll be right over to pick it up." Jonny walks over to her house with a thermos and fills it for Mandy. He's very thankful for her loving kindness and tells her so. He also tells Sadie that Gary is home and getting settled in. She's excited to hear the news.

"I hope to see him and visit with him soon. Please give Mandy my love and best wishes for a speedy recovery."

"I sure will and I'll tell Dad you are looking forward to a visit with him. I know that he has missed everyone here. He'll be excited to visit with you, too. You're a very dear friend. I need to give Mandy a call and let her know that your awesome soup is now ready for her to eat. I'll talk with you later. Bye and thanks again, Sadie."

"Bye, Jonny!"

Jonny walks back to the house with the thermos of chicken soup. He sets it on the counter in the kitchen while he checks to see if his Dad is still upstairs. He doesn't see his Dad downstairs so he sits in the living room while making a phone call to Mandy. His call goes to voicemail so once again he leaves her a message.

'Mandy, I really want to stop by for a visit, if you're up for it. I have Sadie's chicken soup for you, too. Please give me a call so that we can make definite plans. I want to know if you're feeling better. I love you!'

His Dad walks down the stairs looking tired. When they meet up, Jonny asks, "Are you finished unpacking? Are you feeling okay, Dad?"

"Yes, I'm just very tired from the work that I did today. I'm relieved and very happy to be home!"

CHAPTER FIVE
SADIE'S SOUP WARMS THE SOUL

Jonny asks his Dad, "Do you know what you want to eat for dinner tonight?"

"No, not yet. I want to stay in and take a break for the rest of the night. I'm sure that I can find nourishment in the kitchen when I'm hungry. What are your plans? Are you still planning to take soup over to Mandy's apartment tonight?"

"I went over to Sadie's house while you were upstairs. We filled a thermos with the chicken soup for Mandy. Mandy hasn't returned my calls. I hope that she's okay. I might drive over there and check on her. I'll drop off the chicken soup and let her know that it's okay for her to stay home tomorrow."

"Sounds like a good idea. She's a hard worker. It would probably be best for her to get more rest for a quicker recovery. Now that you've mentioned Sadie's soup, I'm feeling hungry." He chuckles. "Do you think Sadie would mind sharing a thermos of soup with me, too?"

"I'll give her a call and ask her or it might be quicker if I walk over to her house with another thermos."

"I'll walk over to Sadie's house to say Hello and ask her myself. Did she have company over? I don't want to intrude. I'll call her first to be sure that she's okay with me stopping for a visit."

"She didn't have company when I was there. Okay, I'm going to take the soup over to Mandy and check on her. I'm concerned. I'll see you later, Dad. Enjoy your visit with Sadie."

"Bye, Jon. Please give my love and best wishes to Mandy. Wish her a speedy recovery."

Jon leaves for Mandy's apartment. His Dad calls Sadie on the cell phone. She answers with a cheerful hello.

"Hey, Sadie? How are you doing my friend?"

"I'm doing very well, thank you. And you?"

"I'd like to visit with you. I moved back to the house today. Is it okay if I walk over to your house for a brief visit? Or would you like to visit here? We can drink a mug of hot cider and chat at the kitchen table."

Sad replies, "I was thinking about eating supper soon but hot cider sounds good. Did Jon tell you that I made chicken soup for Mandy? I have plenty left over. Have you eaten your supper yet? I can bring the soup over and we can eat together. That will give us time to catch up on things. It'll be great to see you again, Gary."

"Sadie, you're such a dear friend. I would enjoy chatting with you at the kitchen table like old times. Whenever you're ready to drop in, the door is unlocked. A definite, "YES" to the leftover soup!" They both chuckle. "Do you need help carrying the kettle?"

"No, I'm good. I'll be over in just a few minutes.

Meanwhile, Jonny arrives at Mandy's apartment. Her door is locked so he rings the doorbell. No one answers the door. He returns to his car to keep warm. He calls her on the cell phone again. She answers with a congested and very sleepy voice. "Hello?"

"Mandy, I'm in my car just outside your apartment door. Are you okay? Is it okay with you for me to come in so that we can talk in person?"

"Oh, yes, give me a minute. I was asleep. I need to grab my robe. I'll be right there."

She puts on her robe and slippers while noticing the time. She didn't know that the time had passed so quickly. She goes to the door and invites Jonny in. They cautiously hug each other but look at each other with smiles and loving eyes.

They walk hand and hand over to the couch and sit down to chat.

"How are you doing, Mandy? I've been anxious to hear from you. I left two messages on your phone. When you didn't return my call, I felt it was best to drop in. I hope you don't mind?"

"No, it's okay, I've been sleeping. I'm feeling wiped out and the cold meds make me drowsy. I didn't hear the phone ringing, I'm sorry." She looks around to try to remember where she left her phone. "Oh, no, Jonny. Looks like I forgot to put it on my nightstand. No wonder I didn't hear it."

"It's okay. I'm just relieved to see that you're surviving. I brought you a thermos of Sadie's chicken soup. Are you hungry? I'm sure that it's still warm and ready to eat."

"Sounds wonderful Jonny. Thank you so much. How's Sadie doing? And your Dad? Let's sit at the kitchen table and chat. Do you want a bowl of soup, too?"

"Sadie and Dad are doing very well. Yes, I'll have a small serving of soup. Dad might be eating supper with Sadie tonight. You probably can't guess what they'll be eating." They laugh.

Mandy says, "But Sadie's homemade soup is the best I've ever eaten. It not only tastes good but it works wonders."

"Make yourself comfortable, sweet one, while I serve the soup. I know where the dishes and spoons are stored. Is there anything else you would like to eat or drink?"

"Yes, I'll have another glass of orange juice. Please help yourself to whatever you want to eat or drink. I'm not very good at playing hostess right now."

"It's fine. I want to tell you before I forget, please don't worry about coming in to the office tomorrow. If something comes up that we can't handle, it'll have to wait or we can contact you via phone or video chat."

Mandy laughs, "I wouldn't want anyone to see me on video chat in this condition. Hopefully it can be handled over the phone or wait until I'm feeling up to driving to the office. I appreciate your thoughtfulness. You know how much I love my job and want to be there. You also know how much I love you and want to be there with you. It's a fact though that I'm very sick. I'm thinking it might be the flu. Hopefully another good night's sleep, cold meds and Sadie's soup will help me to feel much better soon."

They sit at the kitchen table side by side. They eat the soup while they chat and enjoy each other's company.

Back at home, Gary and Sadie sit at the kitchen table while they eat soup, chat and enjoy each other's company. Gary has been away since July so they've got a lot of catching up to do. They laugh and talk about a lot of different topics. Sadie shares the latest news about Charlie and their relationship. She asks about Katherine.

"I don't know about Katherine. I should give her a call. Maybe tomorrow since it's too late this evening. I missed her and hope she's doing okay. I try to give her the space that she needs to heal. I think about her often and would like to spend more time with her. How's your family?"

"My family is doing fine. The little ones are already talking about the holidays. You know how kids are today. As soon as summer is over they start talking about and planning for Halloween." She laughs and shakes her head in disbelief. "It's hard to believe this is the first of October already."

"Yes, Sadie, the time sure does fly during this time of year. I'm looking forward to celebrating the holidays with family and new friends. How about you?"

"The kids are growing so fast. It'll be fun to watch them do their thing. I don't have much say about the things they do. I just try to enjoy watching and taking part in whatever way that they include me. I'm not sure how Charlie celebrates the holiday season. We'll talk about that soon so that we can plan ahead."

"We can still plan on fulfilling our family traditions. You'll always be welcome to join us for our holiday fun and get-togethers."

"Thanks, Gary, I'm glad to hear that. I'm looking forward to celebrating the holidays knowing that things will not change too drastically. There have been a lot of life changes this year. I'm happy to know that those changes will not affect the holiday celebrations. I'll do whatever I can to help make the holiday season a memorable one for our extended families. I still love to cook and bake. I think it's good that we plan ahead as much as possible."

"I agree, but I think we should focus on one celebration at a time. In the past, we celebrated harvest time with decorations. While others decorated with spooks and goblins for Halloween. We opted to decorate for harvest with cute smiley pumpkins and cornstalks with smiley scarecrows. The fun masquerade parties that we hosted in the past seem to be popular. Would you be interested in giving me a hand to put together family fun again this year?"

"Definitely. I'm feeling a little overtired right now, Gary. We can chat about this again soon. I think I'm ready to call it a night and head home. It's been great to see you and visit with you again. Would you like for me to make the coffee and cook you a nice homemade breakfast in the morning? You know, I've really missed doing that for you and Jonny."

"That would be a wonderful blessing, Sadie. I know that Jonny would appreciate his favorite meal. You're a great cook! The coffee is always excellent. I'll be going to bed soon, too. Hope you rest well. See you in the morning."

Gary turns on the security light and watches to be sure that she arrives back at her home safely. She makes it back safely.

He returns to the living room with a cup of hot cider and relaxes in his recliner. As soon as he begins to feel sleepy, he heads upstairs and gets ready for bed. He hears the door downstairs open and recognizes the sound of the footsteps. He knows now that Jonny is home! He decides that they can catch up tomorrow morning at breakfast. The bed is calling him. He's feeling the joy of being home and back in his large bed with family and friends close by. He snuggles in his bed with the joy of knowing Sadie will cook a homemade breakfast for him and Jon once again. Just like old times. He's missed those special moments. He falls fast asleep.

Jonny climbs the stairs quietly not wanting to disturb his Dad's sleep. There's a totally different feeling of love and warmth in the house with his Dad home again. Jon feels comfort by the knowledge. He feels a level of security that wasn't in the house while his Dad was residing at the lake house. He's happy that his Dad his home!

Although Jonny is concerned for Mandy, he needs to get some sleep. Tomorrow is another work day. It will seem strange to work without Mandy by his side. She's been there for him for several months.

He gets ready and crawls into his bed. He's a little restless thinking about Mandy. He can hear a faint familiar sound of his Dad snoring. That's okay with him. He takes a photo from his nightstand and looks at Mandy. 'Good night, my love. Feel better soon. I love you."

Back at Mandy's apartment, her thoughts are with Jonny. She's thankful that he brought her the soup and for the time that they spent together. She's beginning to feel a lot better and is hoping that she'll feel refreshed in the morning.

She looks at his photo on her nightstand and wishes him a good night. She adds an "I love you, Jonny!" She closes her eyes and falls fast asleep.

Sadie's famous chicken soup brought the family together again. It was perfect to nourish and comfort Mandy. Just like old times, it was warmth and comfort to the Young Family.

CHAPTER SIX
CHARLIE'S BIG SURPRISE

Life has a habit of slowing down during the time of transition from Summer to the Autumn season. The temperatures drop and so do our energy levels for a short time. It seems to happen habitually to the people living in the Omaha area. It takes time to switch gears and adjust to the cold weather settling in. But once the transition is complete it seems everyone is revving up for the fun with family and friends that's associated with celebrating the holidays.

Despite the cold weather and feeling a bit run down, Mandy and Jonny have been working long hours in their offices at the Agency. All the businesses are staying strong. Mandy along with both Young men have confidence that the businesses will flourish and prosper over the forthcoming holidays.

They've already shared a few thoughts and ideas about how to make the celebrations bigger and better. They want to share and enjoy the time with Sadie's children just as they have every year. They want to honor Angela by continuing her charity projects for the less fortunate.

They agree not to rush things and take time to enjoy one fun family event at a time. They think it's best to keep communication lines open and flowing as they try to spread their love and joy to the maximum.

At the end of the busy week, Jonny and Mandy reserve a quiet table for two at Ted's Steakhouse. The restaurant serves good food and it's convenient to walk there after work from their offices in the Agency's building.

Jonny gives Mandy a hand with her jacket because he's a gentleman. Mandy smiles lovingly and gazes deeply at Jonny as he playfully wraps her scarf around her neck. Laughter rings out as they try to hug each other. They both bundle up with lightweight jackets, knit caps, neck scarves and gloves before heading out the back-double doors leading to the patio.

As they walk through the patio area to the restaurant, they notice the flowers and bushes in the garden are turning brown now. The gardener has already begun preparations for the cold weather season. He'll surely do a good job giving it lots of TLC again this year.

Mandy and Jonny agreed earlier that It's too cold to eat outdoors on the patio. When they arrive, they see the chairs are tipped toward the tables and there are no tablecloths. They're thrilled to see colorful autumn decorations on the patio. It's decorated with garlands of orange and gold. The twinkle lights are flashing a sparking orange color. Gourds of all shapes, colors and sizes are strategically placed on bales of hay lining the edge of the sidewalk. The inside of the restaurant is also decorated with autumn colors. It looks elegant and it has a lovely relaxing atmosphere. The aroma of hot apple cider fills the air.

The waiter seats them at their table and hands them their menus. They remove their hats, scarves and gloves but decide to wear their jackets a little longer. It's warm in the restaurant but the weather outside was colder than they expected. They order two cups of hot apple cider. Jonny orders his usual steak and potatoes. Mandy chooses the clam chowder and a sandwich. While their meals are being prepared, they touch hands across the table and chatter lovingly and softly about their ideas for a fun weekend.

They finish eating their meals and agree to visit with Gary and Sadie tonight for a family discussion. Now that they've seen these decorations, they're excited to decorate their own places. They'll share their creative ideas for autumn and a fun Halloween theme. This weekend should be perfect for outdoor activities.

They walk back to the parking lot by the Agency building. Jonny says, "We'll meet back at Dad's house. See you soon, love you!"

She replies, "See you there, love you!"

When they arrive, they hear Sadie and Gary in the kitchen. Sadie prepared a delicious dinner for the two of them. Now they're busy clearing the table, washing dishes and chatting.

As they walk toward the kitchen, Jonny and Mandy jokingly call out, "Hello, is anyone home?"

They greet each other with smiles and hugs. They're excited to share about their plans for this weekend. After they are sitting comfortably at the kitchen table, Gary says, "I really like the news that Sadie shared with me at dinner." He looks at Sadie and asks, "Will you please share the fun news with Jon and Mandy?"

"Sure! Today, Charlie and I met for lunch and discussed our weekend plans. He told me that his Uncle Pete owns a farm about a half hour from here.

For the past few years, his uncle has opened part of it to the public. He made it possible for families to come out for hayrack rides and buy pumpkins from his patch of land. His Aunt also opened a store that sells decorations and food items like apple cider. Charlie told me that he thought my grandchildren might enjoy the experience. Charlie invited the whole family for a fun family get-together this weekend. Are you interested in joining Charlie and I as well as my grandchildren?"

Mandy and Jonny were so excited that their faces lit up. Mandy replies, "This will be a new experience for me. What about you, Jonny?"

Jonny says, "Yes, that would be a great place to buy the items we were discussing at dinner. His farm will also be a great place to start in finding decorations for your apartment. Dad, are you interested in going out there tomorrow, too?"

"Yes, sounds like it will be a fun family time. Charlie will drop by this evening with the driving directions and more information."

Sadie says, "I'll go home, freshen up and call my children. This is short notice but it could be a great time for the kids to get out and enjoy the autumn weather. I'll be back soon."

They all say, "Bye, Sadie!"

Sadie freshens up and changes into a new outfit. She's excited to see Charlie, tonight. She calls her son and then daughter to invite them and the little ones to the outing tomorrow. Her son and daughter are thrilled for their kids to spend time with their Nana but the adult children must work. The grandchildren have their allowances to pay for items at Uncle Pete's farm. Sadie tells them that she'll call again tomorrow to finalize the details of their plans.

Sadie walks back to Gary's house. Charlie will arrive there at any moment. Once inside, she notices that they've moved out of the kitchen to the living room. She offers, "How about a cup of fresh coffee. Or, would you like a cup of hot apple cider?"

Gary replies, "Maybe later, Sadie, come on in, relax and visit with us."

When the doorbell rings, Jonny jumps up and opens the door. Charlie has arrived with a package of fresh baked cinnamon rolls from the local bakery. He wanted to bring a fresh from the oven treat for Sadie and family.

Sadie meets him and greets him with a warm hug. They talk softly as they walk toward the kitchen. She sets out a tray with forks and plates. When she offers Charlie a cup of hot apple cider, he says, "Yes, thank you! That will be delicious with the cinnamon rolls. Do you want to check with the rest of the family?"

"I offered coffee or cider a short time ago and they wanted to wait. But they might change their minds now that you brought fresh baked rolls to eat with it. It feels like a celebration tonight. Let's ask again, shall we?"

They chuckle and stroll into the living room. Everyone is looking relaxed. Gary is on the phone with Katherine. He's inviting her to go to the farm with them tomorrow and to his house tonight for a family visit. She declines the invitation for tonight because she made prior plans with her friends. She tells him that she will call him tomorrow morning to discuss the other invitation. He's feeling sad but tries not to show it.

Sadie and Charlie lit up the room with their offer to serve the rolls with coffee or cider. They moved to the kitchen table where it is warm and cozy. Sadie brews a fresh pot of coffee and Charlie heats up the apple cider from the refrigerator.

While enjoying their hot drinks and fresh rolls, they chat and laugh about Pete's Pumpkin Patch. Sounds like tomorrow will be a fun family adventure. Charlie printed copies of the driving instructions for each driver. He shares, "I'll drive my old pickup truck. That should give us enough room to haul the pumpkins and other items back home from the farm."

Jonny says, "That's a great idea, Charlie. Mandy and I discussed earlier about buying decorations for her apartment and maybe decorate the house for her Mom and we'll decorate with my Dad here. We're looking forward to buying some things at the farm for our projects."

Charlie shares, "My Uncle and Aunt have promised to show us a good time after they close the farm to the public. They suggest that we arrive around 3 or 4 while it is still daylight. It'll be easier especially for the children to get a good look around the farm and enjoy the pumpkin patch activities. Aunt Polly suggested that we use their guest cabin on their farmland. We can use it to freshen up or warm up by the fireplace inside. There is a campfire setup by the cabin with a picnic table. Sitting outdoors under a full moon tomorrow night sounds heavenly. Both Aunt Polly and Uncle Pete will join us for roasted hot dogs and toasted marshmallows as well as s'mores by the campfire."

Sadie says, "I don't want to keep the grandkids out too late even though it's a Saturday night. Lots to think about and plan around but I love it, Charlie. Sounds like a fun family time to me. I'll let my children know tonight what we're planning for tomorrow."

They're all smiling and thinking it'll be lots of fun to go to Pete's Pumpkin Patch tomorrow. They talk amongst themselves about transportation.

Charlie says, "Let's all meet at the guest cabin on their farm at 3:00pm tomorrow. Aunt Polly said she will have the door unlocked and preparations made for our arrival. I just need to let her know which time will work for all of us."

They all nod in agreement, it's all settled then.

Mandy tells Jonny, "Excuse me for a minute please. I want to give my Mom a call and share our final plans with her. I think she'll enjoy the Pumpkin Patch activities. It'll do her a world of good to get out in this beautiful weather and see the beauty of nature in autumn. It'll just take a minute."

"Of course, Mandy! You can use my office down the hall if you want privacy."

"Thanks, Jonny! I'll be right back!"

Charlie says, "I'm going to take off now so I'll say goodbye, Mandy!"

Sadie says, "I'll say goodbye, too! I need to go home and call my kids to make the final arrangements for tomorrow."

Mandy tells Charlie and Sadie, "Have a good night. It was great to see you both again. I look forward to spending time with you tomorrow! I'll see you there! Thank you for everything." She walks down the hall to Jonny's office and closes the door.

Charlie and Sadie say good night to Jonny and Gary and leave. They walk together to Sadie's house for a friendly visit.

Within a few minutes, Mandy returns to Jonny's side. She explains, "Mom did not answer her phone so I left her a voicemail message. I shared our plans and encouraged her to join us tomorrow."

Gary adds, "She'll call me back tomorrow morning to give me her answer. I hope she will join us. I enjoy her company and I love to see her smile."

Mandy says, "It's late and I'm feeling sleepy. I'm going to leave for home now so that I'm rested for our new fun adventure. Goodnight, Jonny, I love you! I'll call you in the morning."

Jonny walks with her out the door to her car. "Good night my darling Mandy. I love you. Drive safe."

They exchange hugs and kisses and he stands out by the street watching her drive away.

Jonny and his Dad call it a night as well since they are both tired. They exchange "good night and love you" as well as their excitement about a new adventure.

CHAPTER SEVEN
FAMILY BLESSINGS

Charlie drove out to the farm last night. He met with his uncle and aunt to finalize the family party plans. They coordinated a time schedule and a menu. He spent the night in the guest cabin. He wakes up early in the morning and eats breakfast with his family at their farmhouse.

While his aunt and uncle are busy with their chores and their pumpkin patch, he prepares the guest cabin for the party. He wants feel secure that everyone will have a safe and happy time there. He decorates the two picnic tables with autumn color tablecloths which belong to his Aunt Polly. Sadie and her kids have a special place in his heart. They're on his mind while he's creatively setting up the campsite. He hauls firewood over to the fire ring. He clears away twigs by the log benches set up for the kids to sit on by the campfire. After he preps the cabin and yard, he takes off to the grocery store and buys most of the items on the list. Some of the items are available at Aunt Polly's craft and gift store by the pumpkin patch. He's very happy to be associated with the Young family. He takes extra time and special care to make it a special day for all of them. This idea was on short notice but hopes it will be a memorable fun filled day!

Katherine wakes up mid-morning and listens to Mandy's voice message. She wasn't up for spending time at a farm today. The voicemail stirred her desire to spend time with her daughter. Mandy convinced her to join them for a fun day of celebrating. She calls her daughter and accepts the invitation. As promised, she also calls Gary and tells him that she will join them at the farm/pumpkin patch today. He offers to give her a ride there and back. She'll be ready to go at 2:30pm.

Sadie arranges for her grandchildren to arrive at her home over the lunch hour. After work, their parents will drive out to join the party and take their children home. She calls Charlie on his cell phone. She asks, "What food or beverage should I bring to the festivities?"

Charlie replies, "Not a thing. We've got this covered. I'm out at the cabin right now prepping for our family get-together. I'll be here waiting for you. Drive safe! It's a beautiful day here at the farm. The leaves are a beautiful array of autumn colors. The weather is perfect for outdoor activities. I look forward to seeing all of you at three o'clock."

"Jonny and Mandy shared their plans to drive out to the Pumpkin Patch store a little earlier. They want time alone to shop for their decorations and check out the place. They plan to arrive at the guest cabin on time for our get-together."

"My uncle and aunt plan to give us free admission at the gate this afternoon. I'll let them know and I'll be on the outlook for their arrival. Or, perhaps you can share that fact with them before they leave there."

"I'll share the news with them before they leave the house. Thanks, Charlie! Your aunt and uncle sound very loving and generous. I look forward to meeting them today!"

"I better get off the phone now because I'm helping them with a few chores. See you soon."

Okay. My grandchildren will arrive shortly and we'll leave here around 2:15 or so. I want to give myself enough time to find the place. I've never driven out that way before. I'm glad you gave me a detailed map with driving instructions. See you there!"

Sadie is currently in Gary's kitchen preparing lunch for them and her grandchildren. She ends her call with Charlie and shares the conversation with Gary and Jonny. She hears cars nearby the area of her house. She leaves the kitchen in a hurry and heads out the door to check her driveway. Her children arrive and drop off her grandchildren. Hugs, laughter and chatter express their excitement. She ushers the 3 grandchildren over to Gary's house where she has lunch ready and waiting. They're happy to see Jonny and Papa Gary, too! Sadie's grandchildren are Mike (7), Marie (5) and Tanya (3). Mike and Marie are sister and brother. Tanya is their cousin. They're great kids and the adults will enjoy sharing a fun time with them.

Sadie invites everyone into the kitchen for lunch and serves them. They chat and share their anticipation for the fun they want to have this afternoon and evening. Jonny rushes through his meal. He says, "Thanks, Sadie. The meal was delicious as usual. We'll see you at the cabin later this afternoon. I'm going to pick up Mandy now and drive out to the Pumpkin Patch. We want to get a head start on our shopping before the family get-together begins. Good bye everyone. See you there!"

They all say goodbye to him! Gary also rushes through his meal knowing that he will drive out to pick up Katherine soon. Sadie clears the table and cleans the kitchen while the kids finish eating. They tell Papa Gary goodbye as he heads out the door. Sadie takes the kids back to her house so they can freshen up and prepare to leave, too.

After they freshen up and gather together their personal items, Sadie sits down with them on the couch in the living room. She uses the information that Charlie printed to share with them. Since this is a new adventure, she wants to be sure the kids understand what will be happening. She encourages them to stick close by. She warns them of the dangers and her desire to keep them safe. The kids are all ears. You can see the joy on their faces. They love their Nana and all are happy to spend time with her. Although, Tanya is only 3 years old, she listens intently with a big smile! They exchange hugs and love.

Sadie says, "Are you all ready to go and have some family fun?" All 3 cheerfully say, "YES!" Sadie helps them get settled in her car. She buckles their seat belts and places Tanya in a car seat. She's expecting a half hour drive per the driving instructions. About 20 minutes later, her car is not acting right. She's out on a narrow country road but manages to safely pull off to the side. She steps out and looks around and realizes she has a flat tire. *Terrible timing!* She has a spare in the trunk but she has not changed a tire by herself in years. She decides to call Charlie for help.

"Charlie? I have a problem. We were on our way to the farm but we're sitting on the side of a country road with a flat tire."

"Where are you?"

"According to your map, I'm about 10 minutes away. I'm sitting on 'Old West Rd' and 'Miller's Lane' is the next cross street. The main highway is a couple of miles behind me. You can't miss me parked on this narrow country road.

"Say no more, Sadie, I'm on my way! We can get the spare put on in no time."

Charlie jumps into his truck and practically flies down the road to help rescue her and the kids. When he arrives to the location where Sadie is stranded, he sees another car parked behind her. It's Gary and Katherine and they are happy to see Charlie. He's in better shape to change the tire for Sadie. They offer to help with the kids by driving them the rest of the way to the farm. The kids are happy to see Papa Gary and are excited to go for a ride in his car. Charlie assures them that they'll be back at the cabin with them soon.

Sadie transfers the car seat for Tanya. She secures the other two as well in the back seat. Gary and Katherine arrive safely at the cabin with the kids. The door is unlocked. They enter to check out the accommodations. The area is beautiful outside but inside is luxurious. They decide to sit outside on folding chairs that Charlie set up for them earlier in the day. The kids are running around laughing as well as burning off some pent-up energy,

Mandy and Jonny arrive at the cabin a few minutes before three o'clock. They're surprised and happy to see their parents laughing and playing with the little ones. They say hello to the kids. They each greet their parents with a hug. Gary shares the story about Sadie's flat tire. He assures them Charlie is strong enough to get the job done. Just about that time, they hear Charlie's truck and Sadie's car pull into the parking lot in front of the cabin. Charlie escorts Sadie around the side of the house where the rest of the family has gathered in the backyard and picnic area. They're feeling great relief that Charlie could save the day.

In the distance, they hear a strange chugging sound heading their way. Everyone stops what they're doing and stares off in that direction. They all start laughing and the kids are jumping up and down with joy. It's Uncle Pete driving his tractor pulling a wagon. He stops the tractor a short distance away and steps off to chat with Charlie. He asks all of them to gather around Charlie. Uncle Pete wants everyone to hear.

Uncle Pete explains to the group that he brought the hay wagon to transport them to our farmhouse. It'll be fun for the kids to get a tour and visit with the animals that we keep in our petting zoo. Then I'll transport all of you to the Pumpkin Patch where you can each hand pick the pumpkins that you want to keep. There are other fun activities planned for you there, too. Don't worry about admission. I will close the business down around five o'clock tonight to give all of you more freedom to enjoy your new adventure. Afterwards, Aunt Polly and I will drive everyone back to the cabin. We'll build a campfire and have a lot of family fun together. Are there any questions?"

Sadie speaks up and asks, "What time will you bring us back to the cabin. My children will drive out to pick up their kids. I need to give them a call so they can join us in time for the campfire fun."

"Aunt Polly and I planned on getting together by the campfire around 6:00pm. The sunset will be lovely around that time and there's a full moon tonight. Does that time sound okay with everyone?" They all agree that should be a fine time for a campfire.

Uncle Pete encourages everyone to load up in the wagon now. Take a seat on the hay bales. We've covered them with woven blankets to help protect your skin and clothing. It might be a good idea for the three little ones to take a seat at the back of the wagon. They'll be more comfortable there. After everyone is seated comfortably, he tells everyone to hold on. He'll drive slow and easy but it can be a bumpy ride at times.

It's a quick short trip in the wagon to the farmhouse. He parks the tractor with the wagon securely by the walkway leading to the front entrance. His passengers get out of the wagon safely. He ushers them through the front door to briefly meet Aunt Polly.

The farmhouse has been renovated and upgraded with many modern conveniences. Everyone is impressed by what they see. Aunt Polly greets the group with a cheerful hello and smiles. "I'm looking forward to our get-together tonight by the campfire. We can hopefully visit and get know each other. I'm so happy that you were able to come out and have a fun time here."

"Everyone is happy to be here and they express thanks to Aunt Polly and Uncle Pete. With that, Pete tells Polly, "I'm going to show them around the barnyard. The kids can visit the animals in our petting zoo. After we're done here, I'll drive them over to the Pumpkin Patch. By that time, we'll probably see you there."

"Yes. I plan on returning to the store at the Patch soon. I needed a little break. It's been a busy day. The weather is perfect for families to enjoy outdoor fun and autumn blessings."

CHAPTER EIGHT
UNCLE PETE'S PUMPKIN PATCH

Sadie says, "Very nice to meet you Polly. Thank you for your generosity and hospitality. My grandchildren are so excited to be here. Their eyes are big with wonder. It's a beautiful fun place that you have here."

"It's great to meet you, Sadie. Charlie told me lots of wonderful things about you. I feel like I know you already. OH, before I forget, I want the ladies to know that I printed a menu and a list of food supplies that are available in the cabin's kitchen. I also have a slow cooker set up with beef stew for a hardy meal. Please help yourself to anything that you need for tonight's meal. I'll bake fresh biscuits to eat with the stew after closing time at the Pumpkin Patch. Fellas, you are welcome to help yourselves in the kitchen, too."

Sadie adds, "That reminds me, I need to text my children and let them know when dinner will be served. They're going to join us for the meal and take the children home before their bedtime."

Sadie continues, "Charlie, please keep an eye on Tanya while I take time to text Michael and Amelia?"

Charlie replies, "Sure thing." He stoops down and asks Tanya, "Would you like to take ride on top of my shoulders?"

Tanya asks, "Are you my Papa, too? Yes, you can pick me up like Daddy does."

Charlie and Sadie chuckle at her sweetness. Charlie asks Sadie, "Is it okay with you? Can she call me Papa Charlie?"

Sadie smiles at him and says, "That's okay with me." Sadie sends out her text to her children saying that the Campfire and meal will start at 6:00pm. They're welcome to arrive at any time.

Tanya squeals with delight as she sits high on Charlie's shoulders. She lovingly says, "Thank you, Papa Charlie. This is fun!"

Michael and Amelia reply to Sadie's text. They both plan to arrive with their spouses after work.

Uncle Pete gives Aunt Polly a kiss on the cheek and says, "We'll go now before we run out of time. I think the kids are anxious to see the animals."

Polly says, "See you all later. Have lots of fun kids!"

The group exits the farmhouse following Uncle Pete out and around to the barnyard. The kids are so excited they head straight for the baby goats. Jonny has his camera ready to take lots of photos of the family. The rest of the adults are using their cell phone cameras to take videos of the fun time as well.

Mandy and Jonny wander over to a stall to pet and talk to a couple of ponies. Mandy suggests, "Maybe we can go find a livery stable and go horseback riding sometime."

Jonny says, "Maybe in the spring? I think we should take a few riding lessons."

"Okay! That's a deal! These ponies are the right size for Mike, Marie and Tanya. I wonder if they have pony rides here?

"We can ask Charlie."

They stroll over to where the rest of the family are watching the kids play with a few of the small barnyard animals. Katherine and Gary are resting on a bench. Sadie and Charlie are assisting the little ones. Lots of talking and laughing amongst them. Jonny zooms in with his camera to take several photos of happy smiling faces.

Uncle Pete is encouraging the kids to move on to the pumpkin patch for more fun activities. Both kids and grownups are ready to move on now. Uncle Pete shows them a sink with soap and a dispenser with hand sanitizer. He says, "Help yourself to the soap and water or the hand sanitizer if you prefer." They all wash and dry their hands. It's time to return to the wagon. Uncle Pete helps everyone settle in on the hay bales again.

He drives the tractor about a mile away to his Pumpkin Patch. After they step down from the wagon, they form a group. He gives each of them a map displaying the layout and a list of activities that are available there. The Pumpkin Patch area is very impressive. It's bigger and better than they imagined. Uncle Pete says, "I hope you have a good time here at our Pumpkin Patch. I suggest we meet back here in an hour. We'll drive out to the pumpkin field. You might enjoy hand picking a pumpkin that's just the right size and shape." He chuckles and continues, "It'll be fun for the kids to see. We'll offer one free pumpkin to each one of you as a gift, today."

Tanya asks. "What's a punkin?" They all laugh and smile at her sweetness. Her cousin, Marie, is quick to correct her. She tells Tanya, "The word is 'pumpkin'. Do you remember when we made smiling jack-o-lanterns last year for Halloween?"

Tanya says, "No." She blushes and adds, "Show me, Marie."

"I'll show you a pumpkin as soon as I see one."

Mike shows Marie and Tanya the picture of the pumpkin field on the front of the map Uncle Pete gave him. Tanya is excited to see a real one now.

Charlie and Sadie encourage the kids to stay close by and help watch out for each other Charlie picks up Tanya to carry her through the admission gate. Uncle Pete led the group to the admission gate. He spoke quietly to the cashier about giving them free admission. The cashier placed wrist bands on each one.

Once they're inside the gate, Uncle Pete announces to the family group, "Closing time will be at 5:00pm. I'll be walking around here taking care of business until then. I'll meet you back here at the wagon as close to five o'clock as possible. Have fun!"

Jonny and Mandy tells the group, "We came out here earlier to shop at their store. It's lovely with a variety of handcrafted items. There are food and beverage items, too. We bought indoor and outdoor decorations from the store. Do you want to go shopping there? We can take the kids over to the playground and let them play there for a few minutes. If you need more time to shop, we can take a break and find a snack shop."

Katherine says, "I would like to see the store, Mandy! Gary? Would you like to shop with me in the store? I promise not to take too long. I might return another day for serious shopping depending on what I like in there."

"Yes, from what Jon said, I might find a few things of interest. Since our time is limited, we can browse through the store."

Charlie tells Sadie, "I bought a few items in there earlier today. Do you want to look in there or take the kids over for pony rides? I saw it advertised on the map right here."

Sadie replies, "I'll take Mandy and Jonny's offer to play with the kids while we browse through the store with Gary and Katherine. We can take the kids over for a pony ride afterwards. I'll enjoy watching their fun new adventure."

Charlie says, "That sounds like a good plan. Let's join Katherine and Gary in the store."

Mandy and Jonny take charge of the three little ones and they explain what's happening while they walk toward the playground. Right in the middle of the playground is big smiling pumpkin that houses a slide which is the right size for Tanya. There's an opening in the back with steps to climb up to the top of the slide. Mandy monitors Tanya while she climbs up the ladder safely. She quickly walks around to the front. She laughs out loud when she sees and hears Tanya's delight. Marie and Mike laugh, when they see her slide down through the big pumpkin's smile.

Jonny smiles when he hears Marie's laughter while he's pushing her on a nearby swing. He uses his camera to take pictures of the kids and Mandy laughing and playing around. Mike is climbing on a tractor which is available for the kids to play on.

Mandy takes out her cell phone to snap a few random shots.

Charlie, Sadie, Gary and Katherine are walking up to the playground now. They decided not to buy anything at this moment. Carrying packages around the Pumpkin Patch would be inconvenient. Since their time is limited today, they made plans to drive out tomorrow and make their purchases,

Sadie asks the three kids if they would like to ride a pony. They're in agreement. There's not a waiting line which is a stroke of good luck. Charlie and Sadie help the young man secure the kids on the saddles. There's an attendant for each child holding the reins and walking the pony around on an oval shape trail. Jonny takes several pictures with his camera. Sadie takes a video of their pony ride to share the adventure with their parents.

When the kids are done, they're feeling hungry and thirsty. Sadie helps them clean their hands with the sanitizer until they can locate the restrooms. Tanya says, "Nana, I'm hungry and thirsty."

"Let's look on the map. We can find a restroom where we can freshen up. Maybe Papa Charlie can find the snack shop."

Charlie says, "Let's go this direction. According to the map, there is a restroom close to the food court."

Everyone follows Charlie to the food court. Supper is still more than a couple of hours away. Sadie spies the restroom. She asks Charlie to help the boys clean their face and hands. They all take a break and freshen up before checking out the snack shop. Gary offers to pay for whatever food and beverage they want to order. Everyone is grateful for his generosity. After studying the chalkboard with the specials, they decide to buy a bag of kettle corn to share with hot apple cider and apple juice for the kids. They ask for paper cups to portion out a set amount for the little ones. They take a break while they munch on the fresh popcorn. The wonderful aroma in the food court is triggering an appetite for tonight's cookout. They sit and discuss the other activities shown on the map.

After the kids finish their snack and juice, they're ready to move on. The hour has flown by. With only a few minutes left to enjoy the Pumpkin Patch, they stroll through the area. They check out the map and match up the attractions of interest. They're having a good time together and want to visit here another day. They walk through the gate and meet in a group by the wagon. Uncle Pete will drive them out to the fields where the pumpkins are growing.

They step up into the wagon to sit down while they wait for Uncle Pete. His timing is perfect. He walks out of the gate shortly after they're seated and comfortable. He smiles and asks, "Are we ready to go out in the field now? My work is finished here. I asked one of my employees to lock the gates before he leaves. I'm ready to go if you are."

Tanya says, "Let's go see the punkins, okay, Nana?"

Uncle Pete laughs and says, "Okay, Sweetie, hold on, let's go see the 'punkins'." He climbs up on the seat of the tractor and starts the engine. It sputters from the chilly weather but it starts chugging along.

Sadie asks Tanya, "Did you hear Uncle Pete say that we're going to see the pumpkins now?"

"Yes, Nana. When will Mommy and Daddy be here? I want them to see the punkins too."

"They'll be here soon. Don't worry, okay? They plan to meet us here after work. Let me check my phone. There's a text from your Mommy and Daddy as well as one from Aunt Amelia. They plan to arrive at the cabin on time. They said that they can't wait to see us.

Tanya says, "Oh, Nana, look!" She points at the field to the right. Are those real punkins? I see them!"

Uncle Pete stopped the wagon and turned off the engine. He jumped down from the tractor seat to assist his passengers.

"Yes, they're real pumpkins. When we get out of the wagon, I'll help you and your cousins pick out a special pumpkin to take home."

CHAPTER NINE
PRIZE PUMPKINS

As soon as Tanya's little shoes hit the ground, she takes off running toward the pumpkin patch. She stops and tries to hug a large pumpkin. It's so big that she's unable to get her arms around it. Fortunately, Uncle Pete's farmhands have clipped that one from the vine. It's ready to go home with this family if they want it.

Tanya says, "Nana? I love this one. Can this one be my special punpkin to take home. Mommy and Daddy will love it, too."

Sadie replies, "Let's ask Uncle Pete and Papa Charlie." She asks them, "Is it okay if Tanya takes home this beautiful prize? Is there enough room in your truck, Charlie?"

Uncle Pete replies with a chuckle, "It sure is! I'll load it up in the wagon for you."

Charlie chuckles, "Yes, there's room in my truck to haul everyone's prize pumpkin. Let me carry it, Uncle Pete, because it looks heavy." Charlie picks it up and carefully loads it in the back of the wagon where Tanya was sitting.

Uncle Pete tells the group, "My farmhands are harvesting the pumpkins for me. You can see there is a row of pumpkins that have been clipped from the vines. You can choose any of those. If you choose one that is ripe and still attached, I have my trusty clippers on hand. Go ahead and look around. The sun is setting now. It's a beautiful evening with the full moon shining down. As soon as we're done here, we'll make a quick stop at the farmhouse to pick up Aunt Polly. It's almost time to return to the cabin."

Sadie and Charlie choose pumpkins for baking homemade pies. Jonny and Mandy have an idea for decorating with their pumpkins. Katherine, also, picks out a pumpkin for baking pies. Papa Gary assists Mike and Marie while they search for their prizes in the pumpkin patch. The kids need Uncle Pete's assistance with their choices. The pumpkins are still growing on the vine. Mike walks up to him with a smile and asks, "Will you please help us?"

Uncle Pete replies, "Sure, Mike. What do you need?"

Mike replies, "Our pumpkins are still growing on the vine. Will you use your clippers? We want to take them home for our Mommy and Daddy."

"Show me where the pumpkins are growing. I will clip them only if they're ripe enough."

Mike leads the way back to Papa Gary and Marie. He points out the two pumpkins on the ground.

Uncle Pete says, "Great choices, Mike and Marie." He easily uses the clippers on the smaller pumpkins. Uncle Pete continues, "Are you able to carry them over to the wagon?"

Mike replies with his right arm muscle flexed, "Yes, I can. I'm really strong, see?"

Gary says, "I'll carry Marie's pumpkin for her."

Uncle Pete asks Gary, "What about you? Did you find one that you might like to take home?"

Gary replies, "Yes, I found a small one earlier and loaded it into the wagon shortly after we arrived."

He chuckles and says, "Thank you for your generosity and sharing your Pumpkin Patch with my family today." Gary extends his hand to shake Pete's hand.

Pete shakes his hand and says, "My wife and I enjoy sharing our blessings with family and friends as often as we can. It was our pleasure."

Gary looks around and says, "I think we're all done here. Perhaps this would be a good time to return to the wagon. It's a beautiful evening. It's has been a fun day! Are you ready to pick up your wife and take us to the cabin now?"

Pete checks his watch and says, "Yes, let's get everyone together and load up the wagon."

Pete and Gary work together to load up and secure the pumpkins. Once everyone is comfortable and secure, Pete starts up the tractor. He drives to the farmhouse and sees Polly ready to go to the cabin. She has the fresh biscuits and pumpkin pies packed appropriately for the ride in the wagon. Everyone greets her with a smile and big hello.

Pete drives the tractor slow and steady with his precious cargo. When they arrive at the cabin, they notice Michael with his wife, Melinda, and Amelia with her husband, Hugo. They're waiting patiently. Pete stops and parks the wagon close by the cabin. The kids' parents walk over to greet them and give them a hand.

Sadie greets them with a smile and says, "Tanya is all tuckered out from today's activities. She drifted off just a few minutes ago." Sadie giggles sweetly as she touches the little one's forehead.

Amelia says, "It's okay, Mom, we'll let her sleep for a few more minutes while we prepare the meal.

She'll wake up energized and a good mood. I'm glad she had a fun day. I hope to hear all about it."

Sadie says, "Maybe we can lay her on the bed in the cabin. There's a small bedroom just off the kitchen. We'll be able to hear when she wakes up. You can watch the fun on video. We also have pictures to share with you and your brother Michael."

Amelia carries Tanya into the warm cabin and places her on the bed. She hears her mom chatting and laughing with Katherine and Mandy in the kitchen. She joins them. Aunt Polly walks in with her baked goods. She stores the pies in the refrigerator and keeps the biscuits warm in a basket covered with a cloth on the counter next to the slow cooker. She finds a slotted spoon in a drawer stirs the stew. It's well done and ready to eat.

Aunt Polly introduces herself to Amelia with a big smile. Amelia tells Polly, "It's great to meet you. My husband, Michael, is helping the men outside with the campfire.

Marie and her Mom, Melinda are feeling lost in the crowded kitchen. Sadie introduces Polly to Melinda. Melinda says, "My husband Hugo is working outside with the men. It's nice to meet you."

Polly asks Marie, "Would you like to help us prepare the food to set out on the picnic tables? Would you like to carry the picnic supplies? I set up a buffet table next to the cabin wall. We need to set out the paper plates, bowls, utensils, napkins, condiments, buns and other food items on the table. I would really appreciate you and your Mom taking care of that chore, if it's okay?"

Polly gives them a printed list of food items needed from the refrigerator. Marie and Melinda are happy to help with the meal they're preparing to eat this evening. They work together and get the job done in a short time. Polly carries out and places the hot stew on the buffet table.

Melinda tells Marie, "You can take a break while I heat the apple cider. Your dad is outside. You can visit with him for a few minutes. Please be careful and don't get too close to the campfire."

Marie's face lights up with a big smile. It's a beautiful night with the full moon lighting up on their cabin area.

The men are busy taking care of things outdoors. Charlie loads his truck with the pumpkins from the patch. Gary and Pete set up and start the campfire where they plan to roast hot dogs and toast marshmallows for s'mores. Michael and Mike Jr. carry several pieces of firewood from the woodpile to the fire pit.

Charlie and Pete check on the smoker where they've slow cooked turkey legs all day. One of Pete's favorite food this time of year. Pete lets out a big, "MmmMmm! Looks and smells good."

Charlie says, "Yes, it does! I'm hungry and ready to eat. What about you guys?" He introduces Michael and Hugo to his Uncle Pete. He explains, "Michael and Amelia are Sadie's grown children. Melinda is Michael's wife and she's Mike Jr and Marie's mother."

Uncle Pete says, "Very nice to meet you. You have great kids. I've enjoyed their company today."

Gary replies, "I'll go to the kitchen and check on the ladies. Maybe I can help them in some way."

Gary walks in and asks, "How are you ladies doing? Do you need any help? What can I do?"

From the bedroom, a sweet angelic voice asks, "Papa Gary? Mommy? I'm awake. Where's Daddy?" Amelia picks her up off the bed and says, "Daddy is outside. How are you doing little one? I missed you today." Tanya hugs her mom real tight around the neck.

Everyone reassures Gary that everything is ready to be served. Katherine says with a sweet smile, "You can carry this dish of food outside if you want to?

Gary takes it from Katherine with a smile. He gives her a little kiss on her cheek. They all exit the kitchen with the last of the food and the pot of hot apple cider. Amelia grabs the milk for Tanya from the refrigerator on her way out.

The campfire is perfect for Marie and Mike to roast their hot dogs. Michael places a hot dog on a roasting fork for Marie. Mike puts the hot dog on his fork by himself. The three of them sit together on one of the log benches. By the time the hot dogs are done, everything is set up at the buffet table. and ready to be eaten. Time to celebrate!

The kids' parents take good care of the kids and sit with them at one of the picnic tables. Mandy and Jonny fill their plates and cuddle up on one of the log benches by the campfire. Polly offers to serve the beverages. They decide to save the hot cider until after they've eaten their meal. The family enjoys this wonderful day.   The full moon, campfire and refreshing night air is perfect for a fun get-together.

There's plenty of delicious food left over. Uncle Pete calls one of his farmhands on his cell phone. He knows that his men will enjoy eating this feast. In a short time, someone drives up in an old jeep wearing a cowboy hat. Uncle Pete and Aunt Polly give him several baskets of hot food as well as a fresh pie. He'll share it with the rest of the farmhands.

Mike and Marie are finished eating and asking about s'mores. Tanya is not old enough to toast a marshmallow and hasn't eat a s'more before. She asks for a graham cracker. Michael, once again, sits with his kids by the campfire. He places two marshmallows on two long forks. The kids stand back away from the flames. Michael helps them create their s'more treats. He places them on a paper plate for the kids to enjoy.

The rest of the family are anxious to try a piece of Aunt Polly's famous fresh baked pumpkin pies. Aunt Polly also made fresh whipped cream for a topping.

The kids' parents are preparing to leave soon. They want to be home in time for baths and bedtime. The kids are looking tired. They had a busy day filled with fun activities.

Charlie tells the kids, "I have your pumpkins in my truck. I'll try to deliver them to your house tomorrow. I'll check with your parents to find out the best time to drop them off at your house."

Together, Amelia and Michael ask Sadie, "Would it be okay if we packaged a couple of pieces of the pumpkin pie to take home for later? We should head back to town with the kids now. It's getting late for them. It's been a long day for us."

Sadie looks at Aunt Polly who gives her a nod and a wink. Sadie says, "Yes, let's go to the kitchen and package what you want to take home."

On the kitchen counter, there are several packages of to-go containers made of plastic. Sadie says, "I'm sure these containers will work perfectly." The three work together packaging several slices of pie for them to take to their separate homes. They package portions of whipped cream. This is a real treat! They're happy that they can enjoy it later.

They both hug their Mom goodbye and thank her for inviting them to join the fun. They go outside together saying their goodbyes to everyone and gathering the kids for the ride home. The kids are sad to leave but sweetly say thank you with hugs as they say goodbye. They had a memorable fun day at Pete's Pumpkin Patch.

Even the grownups had a fun memorable day. Now, they drink hot apple cider while they sit and chat by the campfire. They're ready to eat pie with homemade whipped cream. Mmmm!! Polly's fresh baked pumpkin pie was made with pumpkin grown in their Pumpkin Patch.

CHAPTER TEN
SPECIAL DELIVERIES

While eating pumpkin pie, and drinking hot apple cider, the family chats about the day and future holidays. Ideas were shared with hopes of a family get-together again soon. The Young family men decide to call it a night. Katherine and Mandy agree that it's a good time to leave for home.

Uncle Pete and Aunt Polly explain they'll need to clean the cabin and picnic area before they return home. Another family from out of town has reserved it for tomorrow. My maintenance crew will take care of the inside early in the morning. We must clean up and secure everything on the outside. Sadie and Charlie offer to help clean up the aftermath of their party.

Aunt Polly says, "I appreciate the offer, Charlie and Sadie. It's not necessary but if you're willing to give us a helping hand, I'll accept. We can get the job done faster and return home earlier."

Gary and Katherine ask, "Do you want us to help, too? We're willing and able."

Jonny and Mandy simultaneously speak up and say, "We can fold the tables and the chairs before we go."

Polly says, "Anything you want to do will be greatly appreciated. Thank you!"

Jonny and Mandy complete the chore in a flash. They ask, "Where do you store them?"

Uncle Pete, "Back at the farmhouse. I'll need to load them in the wagon."

Mandy says, "Jonny and I can take care of that chore." They work together carrying and loading the tables and chairs. "Done." While they were busy with that chore everyone else was scurrying around and getting their chores done, too.

They see Gary and Katherine are ready to leave. They're saying thank you to Aunt Polly and Uncle Pete. Katherine and Polly exchange hugs while Pete and Gary share a hardy handshake.

Mandy walks over to express her thanks to Polly and Pete. Jonny is right behind her telling Pete thank you and goodbye to his Dad.

Charlie says, "I have your pumpkins in my truck. I plan on making a few special deliveries tomorrow. Sadie and I will schedule a time to deliver them. Is that okay?"

The group agrees with Charlie that his plan to deliver the pumpkins is a great idea. The families walk together toward their cars, while Pete and Polly drive the tractor and wagon back to their farmhouse.

Gary drives Katherine to her house. She says, "Thank you, Gary. It was a fun new adventure for me. I had a great time with you and your family. I liked watching Sadie's grandchildren have a good time at Pete's Pumpkin Patch. I enjoyed the special time with Mandy, too! I'm glad she encouraged me to join all of you there. I'll call you in the morning. I'm really tired and need to say good night." They exchange hugs and Gary drives away to go to his house.

Jonny drives Mandy home to her apartment. When they arrive there, they chat for a few minutes in the front seat of the car. Mandy looks over at the backseat and says, "Will you help me bring in a few of these indoor decorations? Most of them are fragile."

"I'll be happy to carry it all in if you want to take the time."

"I don't really have room for all of this in my apartment. I remember the trunk is full of indoor and outdoor decorations from the pumpkin patch. We have items here for several people. Maybe we can make a few special deliveries tomorrow. Is it okay to leave most of these items in your car for now?"

Jonny replied, "Yes, especially the outdoor items. We can share a fun day of decorating tomorrow. Call me in the morning and let me know when you're ready to do this."

They search through the backseat and the trunk for the fragile items. Mandy unlocks the front door and they carry the fragile items inside for safe keeping.

Mandy asks, "Do you want to stay for a brief visit before heading home, Jonny? You look tired. We can spend a few minutes relaxing on the couch. I really enjoy our quiet time together."

"That sounds great. I love holding you in my arms."

They cuddle on the couch quietly not saying a word. Both are smiling and happy. Mandy suddenly giggles and says, "I just recalled playing with Tanya on the 'punkin' slide. She is so sweet. I dream of having a little girl one day. It was fun playing with all three kids today."

"I enjoyed the whole day. I'm glad I brought my camera. I have several great family group photos to share. I dream of having a family with you, Mandy. I really love you." They kiss and hug with the lights turned down low.

Mandy says, "I love you very much! I think we should say good night. I'm getting sleepy."

Jonny says, "Good night! I'll see you sometime tomorrow. Sleep well." He stands up and walks to the door.

She follows him. Neither one wants to say goodnight. They stand in a warm embrace and passionately kiss goodnight. Mandy says, "Drive safe. Goodnight, sleep well. I'll see you tomorrow." Jonny leaves and drives home.

Charlie asks Sadie, "Do you want me to follow you home? You drove here with the kids. Now you're alone in a car with an uncertain safety at night. I care about you."

Sadie replies, "I admit that I'm a little nervous about driving my car with an old spare tire. I would feel safer knowing you are close by. When you're ready to leave, I'm ready."

Charlie walks with her to the car. He says, "I'll give you a call tomorrow. Would you like to join me while I make a very special 'punkin' delivery to Tanya? That will be a priceless moment."

"You know I'd love to make the delivery to Tanya. I'd like to accompany you in your truck during all the special deliveries. I look forward to your call. Good night!"

They share a friendly embrace before Sadie settles in behind the wheel. "Charlie says, "Good night. I'll see you tomorrow." He walks over to his truck and starts the engine. As soon as Sadie drives out and on to country road, Charlie follows. Charlie follows close behind all the way to Sadie's house. When they arrive there, he watches until she's safely in the house and drives off to his house.

Uncle Pete and Aunt Polly are very family oriented. They rejoice that the day with family went well. They hope there'll be many more autumn blessings to share with Charlie and his extended family. They all sleep well after a long day and a new fun adventure at Pete's Pumpkin Patch.

Charlie rises early. His heart is racing as he considers the joy he'll receive today. He's excited about spending time with Sadie and her family. While he eats breakfast, he writes a list on a tablet. He tries to organize a delivery schedule. He has pumpkins to deliver at several addresses. He plans to call ahead to set up the best time. He'll wait to make the calls a little later in the day. It's still too early for most people on a Sunday morning.

He unloads his purchases from the truck. He stores the outdoor decorations and his prize pumpkins on the patio. The box of indoor decorations is placed on the kitchen table. It's mid-morning now which is a good time to call Sadie.

Sadie is in the Young family's kitchen cleaning up after preparing a big breakfast for Jonny and his Dad. She hears her cell phone chime and answers it with a cheerful, "Good morning, Charlie."

He chuckles and says, "Good morning to you, too, Sadie! How are you doing? Are you ready to assist me with the special deliveries today?"

"Yes." She laughs with joy. "I sent a text to Michael and Amelia asking what time is best for us to drop by. They responded by saying anytime early afternoon will be fine."

Charlie says, "I unloaded my purchases from the truck. Will you help me set up my decorations? You're so talented. It'll be fun sharing the time with you here."

"If there's enough time after we make all of the deliveries. Sounds like a lot of fun, Charlie. Will I see you soon? I'm going home to change and freshen up for our outing."

"I'll be there in about twenty minutes. I have items to deliver to Gary and Jonny. That will be my first stop. My first special delivery." He chuckles.

"I'll be ready to go by the time you arrive. See you soon." Charlie says, "Okay! 'bye." They end the call. Sadie tells Gary and Jonny about their plans. She says, "Charlie is on his way here to pick me up. We're going together in his truck to special deliver the 'punkin' to Tanya." They all laugh as they remember how sweet she was yesterday. "We'll also deliver the prize pumpkins to Mike Jr. and Marie."

Gary says, "That sounds like fun. Hope you have a great time with Charlie today."

Jonny says, "Mandy and I plan to meet at her place this afternoon. We bought indoor and outdoor decorations. She's so talented. We want to finish that project today and hope they'll last through the Thanksgiving holiday. She bought lots of beautiful things at the Pumpkin Patch store yesterday."

Gary adds, "Katherine and I discussed going out there again today. She wants to take more time to browse through the store. There were several items that appealed to her. We'll probably spend time together decorating her house."

Jonny says, "Maybe we'll see you at Katherine's house. Mandy bought a few items for her Mom from the store. We'll take them out to her today. We'll be in touch. Have fun, Dad! I bought decorations for our house. Can we plan on decorating together sometime today?"

His Dad replies, "Yes, Jon, that's one family tradition that I hope will continue for years to come. Hope you have a good time with Mandy."

Sadie says, "Charlie plans to deliver your pumpkins when he stops here to pick me up. With that in mind, I'll see you later. I'm going home to get changed and ready to go. He'll be here soon." She walks out the back door to her house.

Jonny says, "Dad, would you like to spend some time now, decorating our place. I'm free for about an hour. Mandy is supposed to call me when she's up and ready for my company."

"This is great timing for me, Jon. I can help you unload the items you have in your car from yesterday. Oh, that reminds me. There's a box of your Mom's traditional Thanksgiving decorations stored down in the basement. She used to decorate with an autumn theme for the Thanksgiving holiday "

Jon says, "I remember that, Dad. She would store those decorations away over Thanksgiving weekend and then bring out the boxes of Christmas decorations. I would prefer to wait until next month to set out her favorites. Is that okay with you?"

"Yes, Jon, let's see what you have in the car that you want to use for now. It's always a good idea to make new memories." They head out to the car to sort through the trunk and unload the new decorations. They work on setting up the outdoor decorations right away. They chat while they make new father and son memories. They, also, laugh and share old family memories.

Charlie honks the truck's horn as he pulls up along the curb. They meet half way across the yard. They're expecting his special delivery. Jonny and his Dad, walk over to the back of the truck. They locate their pumpkins as well as Mandy's and Katherine's special pumpkins. They say, "Thanks, Charlie, for the special delivery. We'll be sure to deliver these two special pumpkins to our ladies. Hope you and Sadie have a fun day. I would like to see the pictures or video of the kids when they receive their pumpkins."

Charlie says, "I'm sure Sadie will take a video or at least some snaps of their smiling faces. I'll let her know that you mentioned it. I'm going to pick up Sadie now. If she's ready to go, we'll make the 'punkin' delivery now." All three men chuckle. "Have a good day. We'll see you later."

Jonny and his Dad finish decorating the front yard. They unload fragile indoor decorations that they'll work on later. Sadie decorated inside their house last year. But now that Katherine and Mandy are in their lives, they also want to include them in their family traditions. They want to make new family memories.

Charlie returns to his truck and pulls in to Sadie's long driveway. She's smiling and ready to go. He steps down out of his truck and walks around behind it. Sadie follows him. She smiles lovingly at him. Charlie finds the gift box of decorations and the prize pumpkins for her homemade pies. He asks, "This box is a gift for you. May I carry it into your house?"

"Yes, of course. I'll carry the pumpkins for my pies. Please set it on my kitchen table. It'll be easier to unpack there." As soon as he places it on the table, she lifts the lid to peek in. She's wowed by the contents. "Thank you, Charlie. Maybe we can unpack it after the deliveries."

"That's a great idea, Sadie! I'll enjoy spending the time with you."

While Charlie drives to deliver Tanya's 'punkin', Sadie calls to let them know they're on their way.

Jonny hears the ringtone on his cell phone. He answers it with a loving greeting to Mandy. He asks her to hold for a minute. Covering the mouthpiece with his hand, he tells his Dad, "It's Mandy. I'm going over to her house now. I'll be back soon. We'll keep in touch, okay?"

"Yes, go have a good time. We're finished for now. I'm waiting to hear from Katherine then I'll be on my way, too."

CHAPTER ELEVEN
SMILE!

Jonny arrives at Mandy's apartment around lunch time. His car is packed with decorations and her prize pumpkin. It's a beautiful autumn day. He rings her doorbell. When she opens the door, Jonny is standing there with the pumpkin in front of his face. They both laugh. They greet each other with loving hugs and kisses.

"Are you hungry, Jonny? Would you like to go out for lunch? Or I can make soup and sandwiches for us here."

Jonny replies, "A cup of soup and a sandwich would be great. Please let me help you prepare it."

They eat lunch and then unpack the car. They happily work and play together until the inside and outside of the house are decorated in a fun way. The decorations on the back patio include a string of golden orange lights. It looks a lot like Angela's patio garden behind the Agency building. They take a break and then drive over to Jonny's house. They know that his Dad and her Mom made plans to shop at the Pumpkin Patch today. Mandy has an autumn gift for her Mom and plans to deliver it later in the day.

On a whim, Gary decides to surprise the family by cooking a pot roast for supper tonight. He locates the large slow cooker hidden away on a shelf in the pantry. Using Angela's favorite recipe, he prepares the roast with potatoes, carrots, celery, onion and spices. He places the ingredients in the cooker and covers it with water. After he puts the lid in place, he turns it on with a timer. It will be tender and ready to eat at suppertime.

Katherine calls Gary on his cell phone. Gary answers, "Hello, Katherine. How are you?" He's happy that they're going out together for another potentially fun time. He enjoys spending time with her. She's a sweet soul and her laughter is contagious. He really cares very much for her.

"Hello, Gary. I'm fine and you? Are you ready to go to the Pumpkin Patch with me today? I'm ready."

Gary replies, "I'm ready. I was waiting to hear from you. I'll be right over. It's a beautiful day to go out with a beautiful lady."

"Oh, Gary, you're a flirt. Thank you. See you soon, then."

Gary arrives at Katherine's house. She opens the door and sees Gary holding her prize pumpkins. She's very excited about baking homemade pies for Thanksgiving Day. She takes the pumpkins to the kitchen and leaves it on the counter. They happily spend the afternoon at Pete's Pumpkin Patch.

Charlie and Sadie park along the curb in front of Tanya's house. They notice the front window curtain is moving. They can see Tanya dancing around. She's says with great excitement, "Mommy? Mommy? Nana and Papa Charlie are here." She prances over to the front door. Her Mom opens the front door and invites them in. Tanya hugs them around the knees. She says, "Thank you, Nana and Papa Charlie for coming to my house. Thank you for bringing my special 'punkin' to my house. I love it."

She turns around and asks, "Do you love my 'punkin', too, Mommy?"

Amelia replies, "Yes, I do, Tanya." She smiles at Charlie and her Mom. She says, "Thank you for delivering this to her today. I'll put it on the kitchen table. She enjoyed the pumpkin patch. She told me all about it. Let's sit at the kitchen table and relax. Would you like a hot beverage? I've got coffee, tea, cocoa and apple cider. I hope you'll visit with us for a few minutes."

Charlie and Sadie agree on a brief visit. Sadie says, "Please, don't go to any trouble. Whatever you're drinking is fine. We won't be able to stay for a long visit. We still need to make a delivery to Mike and Marie today."

"I made hot apple cider in a crockpot for Hugo this morning. He had to take care of an emergency at work. Would you like a cup?"

Both Charlie and her Mom nod in agreement and say thank you. Amelia prepared the table ahead of time for Tanya to draw a smile face on her pumpkin. She's too young to make jack-o-lanterns.

Nana picks up Tanya and holds her on her lap. "Is it okay if Tanya draws on her 'punkin' while we visit and enjoy the cider? I want to take pictures or a video. This is a special moment."

"Yes, I'll sit her up on a booster chair so that she can play easier." She laughs. "You might get a few good snaps from there."

Tanya is thrilled to sit up at the table with her Mommy, Nana and Uncle Charlie. Her mom serves the hot cider in mugs. She serves Tanya a sippy cup with warm apple juice. Tanya picks up her washable markers and picks out green to write her name on the back. Her Mom guides her hand. Nana snaps several cute pics and makes a video with her cell phone.

Tanya asks, "Nana, will you help me draw a big smile face on my punkin? I like to draw smile faces on paper."

"Charlie, will you please take a picture or video of the three of us playing together?" She laughs. "I'm so happy to have this fun time with my family."

Charlie says, "Yes, of course! I'm happy to be here, too." He looks at Amelia and says, "The hot cider is delicious."

Nana moves her chair closer to Tanya. They laugh and play together with deep concentration. Tanya draws brown eyes like hers on the front of the 'punkin'. Nana jokingly suggests drawing red lips. Tanya draws brown lines like hair on top by the stem. Like magic her punkin has a big beautiful smile face. It was all in good fun. Tanya is laughing and happy. She reaches over and gives Nana a big hug. Then she hugs her Mommy tight around the neck.

She says, "Thank you for my beautiful punkin. I love you, Nana and Mommy." She tries to get down from her chair. Nana helps her so that she doesn't fall. Tanya says, "Papa Charlie. Thank you for bringing my punkin home." She gives him a hug and says, "Love you, too."

She walks back to sit up in her chair. She drinks her apple juice while the adults drink their cider and chat. Sadie asks Amelia, "What kind of plans do you have for Halloween?"

Tanya's ears perk up. She says, "Oh, Mommy? Can I show Nana my new princess dress?"

"Yes, I'll go get it so that you can show it to her." Amelia removes it from the front closet. She takes Tanya out of her chair and helps her dress up in the costume. Tanya dances around in it with a big smile. "Do you like my pretty princess dress? I'm going to Halloween with Mike and Marie."

They smile and say yes, "You're beautiful!"

Amelia shares the Halloween plans with her Mom and Charlie. "The local mall sponsors a party for the kids next weekend. Melinda and I decided it would be safer and warmer opposed to trick-or-treating in the neighborhood. It's in the afternoon next Saturday. You're welcome to join us there."

Her mom replies, "I'll think about it. It's supposed to snow that weekend. It'll depend on the weather." She glances over at Charlie and says, "We should make our next delivery now." Charlie nods his head in agreement.

Nana holds Tanya on her lap for a few precious minutes. They give each other hugs and kisses goodbye. Tanya says, "Don't go Nana." Nana replies, "We're going to Mike's and Marie's house to deliver their special pumpkins. We'll see you again soon. I love you."

Amelia and Sadie exchange a hug and a kiss goodbye. Tanya hugs Charlie around his knees. He scoops her up and they exchange a goodbye hug. He tells her, "I hope to see you and your cousins at the mall next weekend. Hope you have a happy Halloween."

She says, "Happy Halloween?" They all laugh. He sets her down on the floor and they walk to the door. Tanya watches and waves at them through the front window as they drive away.

Sadie says, "That was fun, Charlie. Precious memories. Next stop, Mike's and Marie's house."

"Just a short drive from here. It's good they live in the same neighborhood." They arrive and park at the curb. Charlie locates their prize pumpkins from the back of his truck. He carries one pumpkin and Sadie carries the other up the sidewalk which leads to the front door.

Mike opens the door before they reach the porch. He invites them in. Melinda and Marie are sitting and waiting for them in the living room. Melinda says, "Let's set the pumpkins back outside on the front porch. Michael is at work today but he plans on helping the kids one night this week. He bought a pumpkin carving kit with patterns at the Pumpkin Patch. The kids want to make jack-o-lanterns with a fun design. Michael can bring them in later."

Both Mike and Marie hug their Nana sweetly. They also give Papa Charlie a hug. Each one smiles and says, "Thank you for delivering our special pumpkins. We had a fun day at the pumpkin patch yesterday."

Nana replies, "It's our pleasure. We had fun there with you, also! Hope we can do it again next year."

Melinda says to her kids, "Maybe Dad and I will have the day off to enjoy the celebration next year."

Nana says, "We just delivered Tanya's 'pumpkin'. We had a brief visit. I hear you're taking

Mike and Marie to the mall next weekend for a Halloween party. Sounds like a fun time for the kids. She invited us to join her there. It'll depend on the weather."

Mike asks his Mom, "Can I show them my costume?" Marie speaks up, "I want to show them my costume, too."

Their Mom says, "They're hanging up in your closets. I'll help you."

Sadie removes her phone from her purse. She's excited to take pictures of Mike and Marie while they're smiling and happy, too. Mike is laughing while he charges in wearing a Spiderman superhero costume. Marie follows behind in a Cat Woman superhero costume. They laugh and have fun with their Nana while she snaps their pictures. Sadie asks Charlie, "Will you please take a picture of the four of us? I'd like a picture with Melinda and my two grandkids."

Melinda says, "Or we can take a selfie with the five of us together."

Sadie says, "Oh, I wish we had thought of that while we were with Tanya. Maybe next time. That's a good idea, Melinda. Everybody smile and say cheese."

Charlie says, "Perhaps the kids can stand on the porch for a few minutes to get a pic with their pumpkins in the background."

The kids say, "Yeah." Charlie takes a picture of Mike, Marie, their Mom and Nana. Everyone is smiling and happy. They say their goodbyes while they exchange hugs and kisses.

Charlie and Sadie return to the truck and head for home. The temperature has dropped and the sun is setting. They're both cold and hungry. Charlie offers to take her out to eat. She says, "I'm not dressed appropriately for a restaurant. Do you want to go to your favorite hamburger spot?"

"I'll leave it up to you, Sadie. I've had a fun time making our deliveries. I'd like for you to have a chance to sit and relax. I think there's a casual café in this area."

"I know how much you enjoy cheeseburgers, I'm okay with stopping at your favorite place. I like to see you smile and have fun, too."

"Okay. You know, it's just around the corner. It'll be very convenient and good timing. Do you want to eat in or do you want your meal to go?"

"Let's eat in because the food will be cold by the time we drive home."

"Okay." He parks the truck and assists Sadie to the door of the hamburger shop. "It's a lot colder out here than I expected. We can warm up with a cup of hot coffee while we wait for them to prepare our food."

They go in and place their orders. It's not very crowded on a Sunday night. They seek out a quiet table for two and wait for their meals to be delivered.

"This is great, Charlie. May I take your picture? Smile and say cheeseburgers." He smiles and she snaps his picture. She adds, "I've had lots of fun with you today. Thank you for the invitation. I enjoyed being with you while we made those special deliveries."

CHAPTER TWELVE
HALLOWEEN AT THE MALL

Gary and Katherine browse through the store at Pete's Pumpkin Patch. They select their decorative gifts and food items. They visit with Aunt Polly at the checkout stand. He buys one of the items that Katherine was admiring and surprises her with the gift. She graciously accepts it with a thank you and a smile. She leans in with a gentle hug and a kiss.

It's a beautiful autumn day. They take time to enjoy the weather by strolling through the grounds of the pumpkin patch. Gary shares, "Do you like roast beef and potatoes? I wanted to surprise the family with a home cooked meal. I'm cooking a pot roast with potatoes at home in a slow cooker. Would you like to join us for dinner, tonight? It's probably well done by now." He chuckles.

Katherine replies, "That sounds delicious, Gary. You're a man of many talents. I will be happy to join you. Are you ready to leave here? I'm hungry and hope we can eat a meal soon."

"I'm ready to go home. Our kids might still be there. When I spoke with Jon earlier, he said they plan to hang out and play a game or two in the basement. He said he would check on the roast." They load their purchases into the trunk of Gary's car and drive home.

When they arrive at Gary's house, they notice someone set the table for four. Gary's grateful. Katherine and Gary are chilled to the bone as well as tired. Gary brews a fresh pot of coffee and heats spiced apple cider in a small crockpot.

Jonny and Mandy put away their game and head upstairs when they hear the car. She's anxious to see her Mom and Jon is anxious to see his dad. They're also hungry and ready to eat the meal Gary prepared. The four of them work together to serve the food on trays and serving dishes. They sit down at the kitchen table and eat their meal as a happy family. Sadie is missed but they know she's with Charlie and her family.

Katherine says, "Very well done, Gary. It's delicious and very satisfying." Mandy and Jonny agree. Gary says, "Thank you. It's made from one of Angela's favorite recipes. I think she would be pleased."

Jonny adds, "I've been spoiled by Sadie cooking our meals. I think I might want to look at Mom's old recipes. It's probably time that I learn to cook a meal or two. Maybe we can have fun learning together."

Mandy says, "Sounds like fun to me. Mom taught me how to cook a meal or two. I would like learning your Mom's favorite recipes. I want to learn how to cook your favorite meal. That skill will come in handy after we're married.

They chat about their day as well as future holiday plans. Not ready to make a final decision but want to share their ideas. They all want a chance to make new happy memories this year with their new family and friends.

After they finish eating their meal, Mandy gets up and brings in the gift for her mom. She hands it to her while she's still sitting at the table. It's a beautiful thanksgiving decoration for her dining room. There's also a box of maple leaf candy tucked away in the gift box. Katherine is so touched that she wipes tears from her eyes. She lovingly says, "Thank you, my darling daughter! I also bought a gift for you today! I'll give it to you a little later. It's still in Gary's car."

Gary goes out to the car and bring in the gift for Mandy. Her mom gives her the gift. She likes the kitchen towel set with a Thanksgiving theme. The gift box also has a Thanksgiving pattern on a fleece throw for her living room couch. Mandy loves it and tells her mom, "Thank you!"

The hour is getting late and with the early sunset, it's cold outside. Jonny asks, "Mandy I think it might be a good time to take you home. We both must work in the morning. It's been a long busy weekend. I'd like to call it a day."

"I agree with you Jonny. I'm ready for you to drive me back to my apartment. I had a fun weekend. There are a few things that I need to get done around my apartment before bedtime." Mandy tells her Mom and Gary goodnight. I hope to see you again soon. Have a good week." She tells her Mom, "I Love you, Mom!"

Jonny drives to her apartment. She walks Mandy to the door and of course she invites him in. They hang out on the couch with a chance to cuddle up and rest for a few minutes. Jonny offers to help with the chores. After the chores are done, they cuddle up on the couch again. Jonny notices that Mandy has very sleepy eyes. He tells her, Goodnight. I'll see you at the office in the morning bright and early."

"Goodnight, Jonny. I've enjoyed this wonderful weekend with you. I'm really excited about the family plans we're making for Thanksgiving Day. See you in the morning, my love!" They exchange hugs and kisses goodnight at the door before Jonny leaves for his house.

Back at the house, Gary and Katherine are preparing to leave, too. They work together cleaning up the kitchen. Jonny misses them only by a few minutes. Gary walks Katherine to his car. He packs Mandy's gift in the backseat. When they arrive, he walks Katherine to her door and she invites him in. He declines because of the hour and temperature outside. It feels like it might snow. The weather is hard to predict this time of year. He asks for a raincheck. She says, "Of course, I invited you in so that we can talk more about the holidays. There's plenty of time to do that. Thank you again for a wonderful weekend and a delicious dinner, Gary." He replies, "My pleasure. I hope we can get together again soon. Goodnight!" They exchange hugs and a quick kiss at the door.

Gary is anxious to arrive home. It's dark and foggy outside making it difficult to see with clarity. He makes it home safely and feels greatly relieved. Jon and Sadie are home safe and sound.

Sadie is relieved that Charlie will take the flat tire to his mechanic for repair. But when he takes it in, they tell him that he needs to buy a new one. Charlie buys the new tire for Sadie because he cares about her. He wants her to be safe on the winter roads.

Jonny and Mandy have a regular and prosperous work week at the office. Some of the employees are busy making Thanksgiving travel plans while others are hoping to have fun at their

Halloween get-togethers. The holidays can turn into holidaze in an instant.

A blizzard has been predicted for this weekend. Next Monday is Halloween. Lots of people celebrate this day by hosting and/or attending masquerade type parties. For some they follow a family tradition that takes their kids out in their neighborhood on Halloween night. The kids knock on their neighbor's door, while wearing a costume and ask, "trick-or-treat?" They hold out their Halloween themed containers to carry home their treats. There are many other ways that people in this Omaha area might celebrate this holiday. This explains why Amelia and Michael will allow their kids to enjoy Halloween. Wearing their costumes at the mall is a safer environment. Retailers will give them age appropriate treats.

The kids are excited about dressing up in their costumes and attending the party at the mall. Sadie looks forward to sharing this time with her family. Charlie must work at that hour. Business at his pool cleaning company is slow now that summer is over. He still has clients that own indoor pools.

Early Saturday morning, the snow begins to fall in huge flakes. It's a beautiful sight. There's a slight howl in the wind. It's obvious the forecast is right on. The road conditions might spoil travel plans. The mall is located on a main public road which is well maintained during snowstorms.

Sadie prepared breakfast for Jonny and Gary. They're sitting around the kitchen table while drinking a cup of coffee and chatting about the upcoming Thanksgiving Holiday. Sadie shares that today is a Halloween celebration with her family. She tells them about her invitation to go to a mall costume party with her grandkids.

Sadie sends out a text to Michael and Amelia asking if they're still planning to go to the mall. Michael replies, "We don't want to disappoint the kids. The snowfall isn't heavy right now. The wind is really blowing the flakes around though. We'll take a chance unless there's a travel advisory which tells us the roads are not safe. We'll wait and see if it progresses. I'll let you know my final decision in about an hour. Thanks, Mom!"

Amelia replies, "Tanya has her heart set on going to 'Halloween' with her cousins. I agree with Michael. I'll wait to see what he decides to do. The roads in our neighborhood aren't too bad right now. The party is open from three to five. It would probably be wise to arrive early and just plan on staying for a short time. Love you, Mom!"

Sadie returns a text to them, "My pleasure and I Love you! I'll wait for your decision. I don't have any other plans this afternoon."

Gary didn't celebrate any of the Halloween traditions as a kind growing up. He and Angela let the holiday pass while Jonny was growing up. He didn't miss it because a lot of his friends in school didn't observe Halloween.

Sadie hears her phone chime and reads the texts from her two children. They're in agreement about going to the party. The road conditions are safe for the trip to the mall. They're planning to take the kids over for the Halloween party. Michael asks, "Will you be able to safely join us there? They're excited to see their Nana."

She replies to their text, "Yes, the roads are safe around here, too. It's cold out but the snow is beautiful. The sun is shining here. It's a beautiful sight. I'll just bundle up real tight. I'm excited about seeing all of you, too. I'll be there at 3:00pm."

They send her a quick reply, "See you there!"

Jonny and Gary aren't excited about going out and about in a potential blizzard. They're happy for Sadie but concerned about her safety. Gary offers to drive her there. She's grateful that they care. Sadie says, "I believe that I'll be okay with the drive there and home again. If you're interested in going to the mall with me and my family, you're welcome to join us. It'll be fun to see the kids happy and smiling while wearing their cute costumes."

Gary says, "I'll be happy to accompany you. It would give me a lift to hear the laughter and see the smiles. I like being with your family. The kids are great! I'll be glad to drive. I think my car can withstand the road conditions a little better than your smaller car."

Sadie replies, "That's probably true. Thank you for your offer. Will we make it there by three?"

He replies, "Yes. I believe it will all work out fine."

Jonny's interest peaks as he thinks about going to the mall with Mandy. It would also be a chance to do a little pre-Christmas shopping with her. He shares his idea with Sadie and his Dad. They laugh but at least a few people will be doing the same thing today.

He leaves the room and calls Mandy. They discuss the plan and she agrees to go out with Jonny to the mall. She says, "It'll be fun to the see kids in their costumes. I really don't like shopping in crowded stores but It's a good way to find a few good ideas for the people on my gift list."

Jonny says, "They're planning to meet at three so I'll be over to pick you up soon. It's really cold outside."

Sadie leaves to freshen up at her house and to change into a warmer outfit. Jonny and Gary go upstairs to do the same.

Gary and Sadie meet at the car and he drives carefully through the fallen snow to the mall. Jonny picks up Mandy and drives carefully to meet with Sadie and family. They all arrive on time. They see Michael, Melinda, Mike and Marie are sitting in the food court with Amelia and Tanya.

The kids see their Nana and Gary walking toward them. They're so excited. Tanya calls out, "Nana? Papa Gary? I'm so happy you came to Halloween." They greet each other with hugs and smiles.

While Jonny and Mandy are walking toward the group, they hear Tanya say, "Jonny? Mandy? Are you coming to Halloween, too?" They laugh and Mandy replies, "Yes, we heard about your princess dress. We want to see you dressed up in it. When I was a little girl, I dressed up like a fairy tale princess, too."

Amelia says, "The kids are going to get in line and have a little parade with their costumes. It was advertised that it will take place on the first floor only. I think we should walk over with the kids now. They're excited to see the other kids dressed in their costumes, too.   Mike recognized a couple of his friends from school here, too."

Everyone follows Amelia's lead and they walk together as a family group.   After they get in line, Sadie and Mandy use their cell phones to take lots of cute pics. Sadie shoots a video of them while they're marching. They're wearing big smiles. Of course, no one lets the kids out of their sight.

After the little parade, the children walk down the hall and stop at the storefronts which have a Halloween theme.   The employees are wearing fun costumes and makeup which adds fun for the kids. Mike and Marie are thrilled with the treats that they receive. There's a variety of wrapped candy, cookies, and small trinkets. Tanya is getting too tired to walk any further. Amelia picks her up and carries her the rest of the way. Everyone has a good time with lots of laughter and smiles.

CHAPTER THIRTEEN
FIRST BIG SNOW STORM

When they're ready to return home, they notice people in the parking lot are digging out their cars. Michael is not worried about his car but sees that Amelia is parked in a bad place. The snow plow left a mound of snow at the back of her car. Jonny tells Michael and Melinda, "I know that you'll want to get the kids home and out of this cold weather. I can help Amelia dig out her car."

Mandy joins Jonny and they work together in a flash to free Amelia's car from the fallen snow. They also dig out his Dad's car. Michael's and Amelia's families are on their way home. Gary is anxious to drive Sadie home so that she's safe and sound. Jonny doesn't free his car yet. Mandy agrees with Jonny to stay at the mall a little longer. Several shops are having pre-Holiday sales. They want to walk through the mall and check out the sales for gift giving ideas. This is a chance to do a little pre-Christmas shopping.

Jonny tells his Dad, "Please be sure to give me a call if you need my help. I'll be there for you. Please drive safe. I'll let you know when we are on our way home."

"Thanks, Son. I will wait to hear from you. Please drive safe, too! I believe that we'll be fine if the roads are plowed. See you later at home."

Jonny says, "Bye, Dad!"

Mandy also says, "Goodbye. I hope to see you later."

Gary drives Sadie home through the blizzard like conditions. They witnessed several drivers stranded along the road. Tow trucks were on the scene assisting the drivers. The forecast predicts more snow is on the way. Gary calls Jonny to share the forecast update. Sadie also touches base with Charlie. Gary hasn't heard from Katherine all day. He gives her a quick call but she doesn't answer. He leaves a voicemail message requesting her to return the call. She heard about the blizzard warnings so she stayed in. She's busy playing cards in her dining area for a few of her neighborhood friends. Her phone is not close by so she misses his call.

Jonny and Mandy take their time in the large mall. They check out all the shops with sales and take notes for some comparison shopping. They also make notes about gift items that are a good match for family and friends. Several hours pass by while they window shop and purchase a few personal items. Intuition kicks in and they feel it's time to leave the mall.

Jonny digs out the car from the parking lot and drives up to the mall entrance. Mandy is waiting with their packages and feels grateful she didn't have to wait out in the snow or cold car. Jonny and Mandy are both surprised at how much snow is covering the cars parked in the lot. They're thankful for the snow plows that have cleared the lot and main streets. He carefully drives Mandy to her apartment so that she'll be safe and warm for the rest of the evening. They unpack her purchases from the backseat and carry them into the apartment.

She invites him in to rest and warm up with a hot beverage. She doesn't have plans for supper yet. They discuss their options to eat dinner together.

Jonny's phone rings. He answers it and hears his Dad's voice say, "Sadie and I arrived home safely but we're wondering, how are you doing, Son?"

Jonny replies, "We're doing fine. I'm at Mandy's place now. I want her to be safe and warm for the rest of the evening. I'm afraid the snow will continue through the night. It was coming down fast and furious when we left the mall. We're trying to decide on supper. What are your plans? Glad you and Sadie are safe, too."

Gary tells his Son, "We're doing fine, too. Sadie said she'll cook an Italian meat and pasta dish with Italian bread for us tonight. It's a good time to warm up the oven. The aroma of fresh baked bread will be heartwarming. Are you and Mandy interested in eating with us?"

"If we do, I'll appreciate it if you let Mandy stay overnight in the guest room."

"I'm okay with her staying in the guest room. It's Saturday night which is a good time to rest and relax. After supper, you two can watch a movie, TV or play games in the basement. It'll be good for my heart to have family fun fill this big house."

"Thanks, Dad, for understanding how important it is for Mandy to be safe and warm. Let me ask her if she's okay with all of this."

Jonny asks her, "Would you like to eat an Italian Pasta meal with Italian bread? Sadie is cooking for us at my house? Dad says you can stay in the guest room. We won't need to drive in the blizzard again tonight."

Mandy replies, "That sounds great, Jonny. Sounds like a new adventure for us. I'll need to pack an overnight bag. I'll pack it while you finish talking to your Dad."

Jonny says to his Dad, "Okay, you can count us in. We're grateful to both you and Sadie. As soon as Mandy packs her bag, we'll leave here and be there as soon as possible."

"I'll let Sadie know to expect you two. I know she'll be thrilled. She enjoys cooking for a family. See you both soon. Drive safe."

"Bye, Dad! We'll see you soon."

Mandy packs two bags. One is an overnight bag with her personal items and the other is a clothes bag. She's ready to go. Jonny says, "I'll go warm up the car and clear the snow away. You can wait in here where it's warm if you want to."

Mandy replies, "I'm good to go." She reaches out and gives him a hug and kiss. They stand in a loving warm embrace by the front door. The clock is ticking. She goes out the door with him to the car. She stows her bags in the back seat. It doesn't take long for the car warm up. The snow is falling and swirling fast. Clearing the windshield from the outside is almost a lost cause. Jonny is strong and energetic. It's easy to clear the snow away from the tires. They arrive at his Dad's house in a fair amount of time.

The aroma of the Italian meal and bread fills the air. Jonny says, "MmMm. The food smells delicious, Sadie. Thanks for cooking it for all of us." Sadie smiles.

Jonny carries Mandy's bags to the guest room. She follows him and asks, "What can I do to help? The room looks beautiful and everything looks in place. Do you have clean sheets and towels?"

Jonny replies, "Knowing Sadie and Dad, they've probably taken care of what you need. They probably went to work as soon as they heard you would stay overnight in here. They're generous like that." He smiles at her and gives her a kiss. "I'll double check with them. Is there anything else that you might need in here?"

"No, Jonny, I feel very pampered and spoiled already." She gives him a hug and a kiss.

"Do you want to take time to unpack your bags now? Or you can wait until after we eat our dinner. I'm going to double check with Dad and Sadie now."

"That's okay, I'll wait. I'll go with you and we can talk to Sadie and your Dad together."

They walk hand in hand to the kitchen. Sadie is cooking while Gary is prepping the vegetables to make a tossed salad. Jonny asks, "Sadie? Dad? Are the sheets and towels in the guest room fresh for Mandy?"

They laugh. Gary replies, "Yes, Sadie and I did a quick sweep in there. We made the bed with clean sheets and hung up a fresh set of towels in the bathroom. Everything was already clean from lack of use. We worked together to freshen the bedroom and bathroom for your stay with us, Mandy. We're happy to have you as our guest here tonight. We hope you enjoy your stay in our guest room. Let us know if you need anything."

Jonny says, "Thanks, Dad and Sadie. We really appreciate your generous efforts."

Mandy adds, "Thank you for your efforts to make me feel at home here."

Sadie says, "You're both welcome." She smiles and adds, "Supper will be ready to serve in about ten minutes. Are you hungry? This is one of my favorite dishes. I hope that you'll enjoy it."

Jonny says, "Yes, I'm hungry. The food smells and looks delicious." Mandy agrees with Jonny. Jonny asks, "Would you like for me to set the table?"

His Dad replies, "Sadie set the table in the dining room for a nice change. We want to treat our house guest in style. I lit a fire in the fireplace. We will have a cozy ambience for our dining pleasure tonight." He chuckles. "I hope you like it."

Sadie says, "If you want to lend a helping hand, you can find the food we need in the refrigerator. We can use salad dressing and butter for the bread. What would you like to drink with your meal?"

Jonny says, "I'd like to heat up the apple cider. This is perfect weather for a hot beverage. Would anyone else like hot cider?"

They all agree with Jonny. He finds the small crockpot in the kitchen pantry and heats up the apple cider that he found in the refrigerator."

Everything is ready to be served and eaten. Jonny serves the hot apple cider in fancy mugs. Gary sets the salad bowl on the table next to Sadie's basket of hot Italian bread. They're thankful for this delicious meal. They're also glad that they're warm and safe from the blizzard conditions. Charlie was invited for this meal but he was unable to make it. He had a long busy day at work and felt too tired after driving home. He decided to stay home because of the road conditions.

Mandy's phone rings. She checks in her purse for her phone. She looks to see who's calling. When she notices that her Mom is calling, she answers it. She asks, "Mom are you okay?"

Her Mom replies, "Yes, are you okay? I invited a few friends over for a card game today. The time flew by fast. I knew it was supposed to snow today. I was busy inside and didn't notice how much snow had fallen until my friends left to return to their homes. I'm very surprised. I'm glad you're doing okay, Mandy."

Mandy explains to her Mom, "I'm staying the night in the Young family guest room. We're eating dinner now. I'll call you back later, okay?"

"Yes, enjoy your meal. I'll wait to hear from you. I'm not going anywhere tonight. Love you, bye!"

Gary is also concerned about Katherine. He asks Mandy, "How is your Mom?"

"I think she's okay. She spent the day inside playing cards with friends in her neighborhood. They lost track of time and didn't pay attention to the weather. She's surprised by the snowfall and blizzard conditions."

"I'd like to call your Mom for a chat after we're finished eating, too."

Sadie says, "I baked a fresh peach cobbler today. It's still warm in the oven. Would anyone like a slice?"

Gary says, "I'd like a piece of peach cobbler a little later, if that's okay? I'm full from eating this delicious meal." Jonny and Mandy nod in agreement. They also offer to clear the table and clean the dishes. Jonny says, "You two deserve a break. I've got this covered. The fireplace is crackling and looks cozy in the den. You should sit back and relax at least for a few minutes."

Sadie says, "I'm going to go home and call Charlie. I want to share the day with him and find out how his day is going. I'll return to enjoy pie and coffee with you later, if that's okay."

Gary replies, "It's perfectly okay, Sadie. I wish Charlie could join us, too."

Sadie replies, "Maybe next time." She gets ready to step out the door when she sees the snow is a foot deep in her driveway and walk area. It's dark and cold. She reacts with a big heavy sigh and says, "OH, NO!! I sure didn't expect the snow to drift in here so deep."

Jonny says, "Why don't you go ahead and make your call to Charlie. By the time, you've completed your phone visit, I'll have a path cleared to your door using our snow blower. It'll be time for coffee and cobbler by that time, too." He smiles. "My muscles are probably going to be sore tomorrow. I've been shoveling a lot of snow today."

Sadie says, "I really appreciate it, Jonny. I'll make my call in a living room recliner out of your way. I don't want to be a bother."

Gary says, "This seems like a good time for me to call Katherine."

Mandy says, "It's okay, I'll call her after we eat Sadie's cobbler. I would like to help Jonny. I don't think there's anything I can do. I'll bundle up and check with him outside."

Gary says, "He'll probably enjoy your company out there. Bundle up tight because it's cold and windy. I'll sit here by the fireplace and visit with Katherine on the phone."

"Okay, enjoy. I'll see you later." Mandy goes outside where Jonny is using the snow blower to clear a path to Sadie's front door. He finished her sidewalk and is clearing her driveway. Mandy cannot resist making a lightly packed snowball and tossing it at Jonny. She misses on purpose. She got his attention! He turns around and laughs at her. When he's finished with the snow blower, he turns off the engine. He picks up a handful of snow, packs it lightly and tosses it at Mandy. They both laugh and seriously begin to play the game. They have their first snowball fight!

CHAPTER FOURTEEN
GREAT WAY TO START THE DAY

Jonny did a good job clearing a path for Sadie. The snow storm has finally stopped. There's still a problem with blowing and drifting snow. He returns the snow blower to the storage shed. He finds the salt container and sprinkles it on Sadie's driveway and walkway. He'll need to add that item to their shopping list. Jonny and Mandy shake off the snow from their hats, gloves and jackets while lightly stomping off excess snow from their boots.

They enter the house through the garage door, which leads to a hall with the utility room off to the right. They hang up their wet jackets, hats, scarves and gloves on a drying rack. They're shivering and cuddling up trying to feel warm again.

Jonny says, "Let's go stand by the fireplace."

Mandy says, "Good idea!"

They see that the den is empty. Standing by the fire for only a few minutes warms them from head to toes. Jonny says, "I wonder how Dad and Sadie are doing?" They hear voices coming from the kitchen.

Mandy reminds Jonny about their plans to eat cobbler and drink coffee.

Gary and Sadie both moved to the kitchen. He finished his visit on the phone with Katherine. Likewise, Sadie finished her phone visit with Charlie. She made the coffee and set the table with forks and saucers.

Jonny and Mandy walk into the kitchen just in time. Sadie is pouring the coffee in fancy mugs. Gary is serving slices of cobbler on the saucers.

Jonny says, "I cleared the driveway and walkway for you, Sadie. The snow is not falling anymore. We'll need to be careful around the blowing and drifting snow."

"Thank you, Jonny. You know I appreciate your hard work. I'm relieved that it will be safe for me to walk home soon. Are you two ready to join us?"

While they take a seat at the table, they both nod in agreement. The cobbler and hot coffee is delicious and warms the soul as well as their cold hands.

Jonny says, "We need to add salt to de-ice the drive and walk ways to our shopping list. I just used the last of the container that was in the storage shed."

Gary says, "I'll pick it up at the hardware store tomorrow, if we're able to get out and about."

They chat about this and that while they enjoy their family time. Mandy is looking and feeling sleepy. Jonny asks, "Mandy? Are you okay? You look sleepy. You know it's okay for you to retire to your room at any time. It's been a busy fun filled day. I understand that you're tired and need to sleep."

Mandy replies, "I'm okay, Jonny. I'm feeling sleepy but I'd like to take a hot bath before bed, if that's okay?"

"It's perfectly okay, Mandy!"

With that, she stands up with her cup and saucer in hand. She takes them over to the sink and rinses them before adding them to a rack in the dishwasher. She looks around the room and collectively says goodnight to everyone. She reaches over to give Jonny a hug.

He says, "I'll walk with you down the hall to your door." They both smile.

Mandy says, "Goodnight Gary and Sadie. I hope you both sleep well. Thank you for allowing me to stay overnight. I've greatly enjoyed the family time that we've shared."

Gary says, "Sleep well, Mandy dear! If you need anything, let one of us know. We'll help in any way that we can."

Sadie says, "I'm planning to cook a big breakfast in the morning. Do you have a special request?"

Mandy replies, "No, thank you. Whatever you cook, will be fine with me."

Sadie says, "I hope you sleep well and we'll see you in the morning." They exchange a gentle goodnight hug.

Mandy and Jonny walk down the hall to her room. They stand outside her door while they share a loving embrace and several good night kisses.

He says, "Be sure to let us know if you need anything. I'll be more than happy to help you. I love you very much. Hope you sleep well. I'm already anxious to see you again in the morning. This has been a fun new adventure."

She replies, "Everything is perfect. I'm sure I'll sleep very well. At my apartment, I can hear traffic noise and the noise that my neighbors are making in the night. It's very quiet here at your house. I've had a lot of fun today with you and your family. She gazes lovingly in his eyes and reaches up to give him another kiss. He leans in for one last goodnight kiss. They simultaneously say, "Good night! See you in the morning!"

She opens the bedroom door and closes it ever so gently. She locates her bubble bath liquid in her overnight bag. After soaking and relaxing, she dries off and dresses in her nightgown. She sets an alarm on her cell phone so that she doesn't oversleep. It's so quiet and warm. Everything is perfect in her room for a good night's sleep. She feels safe and secure with Jonny in the same house.

When Jonny returns to the kitchen, his Dad says, "Sadie asked me to tell you good night. She wanted to wait but felt you two need time together. She'll be back in the morning to cook a big breakfast for us. She asked me if Charlie can join us for breakfast. I said, "Yes. He's like family and I think he'll enjoy one of Sadie's home cooked breakfast. She's in the mood to cook a big breakfast. We're really blessed that she enjoys cooking for us. She's really a great cook and baker!"

Jonny says, "I like Charlie. He feels like an extended member of our family. It'll be fun. What about you, Dad? We can plan on breakfast being a brunch for all of us. You could call and invite Katherine. She's part of our family, too."

His Dad replies, "It's too late to call her now. I'll send her a quick text with an invitation to join us tomorrow morning. She can reply in the morning when she wakes up. That will be a nice surprise for Mandy, too."

Jonny says, "I'm ready to go upstairs to my room. I'm feeling several sore muscles and back pain from all the snow that I've moved around today. I'm going to take a hot shower before bed. That might relax a few tight muscles." He smiles at his Dad. "I'll say good night to you. Hope you sleep well. I'll see you in the morning."

His Dad says, "Good night, Son. I'm going to relax by the fireplace in the den for a few minutes before I go upstairs to bed. Sleep well!"

Jonny takes a hot shower and is ready for bed. He smiles inside and out as he thinks about Mandy being in the house. He falls fast asleep.

Gary sits by the fireplace and gazes at the flames. Listening to the crackling is comforting and watching the flames are a bit hypnotic. He gathers his thoughts and relives the memory of meeting Angela as well as the day they first moved into this big house. He reflects on her illness and the day she passed away. There are a lot of happy and sad memories in the house. Time is short and life seems harder emotionally during the holidays.

He thinks about his desire to continue family traditions but it feels like the right time to make new family memories. He's happy that Jonny found his true love. He wishes Angela could be here to enjoy this happy time with them. He misses Angela but he's thankful for the life he shares with his son.

He dries a few tears from his eyes while walking over to the fireplace. He uses the poker to break down the fire and successfully extinguishes the flames. He mashes down the ashes to be sure the fire is out. While he walks up the stairs, he listens to make sure everything in the house is calm and secure. He manages to fall asleep and sleep well through the night.

Mandy's phone alarm rings at 8:00am. She silences it quickly so that it doesn't disturb anyone in the house. The house is quiet still. She doesn't feel pressured to jump right out of bed. She's wide awake because she rested very well. She's excited to see Jonny and the rest of the family. The thought of seeing him makes her heart race. With that thought, she promptly gets up out of bed. She searches through her bags to set out the items she will need to dress for the day.

Sadie sends Gary a text because it'll be less disturbing than a phone call. The text reads, "Charlie just arrived here, "Can you send me a text after you read this message? I'd like to know when you're ready for me to start cooking breakfast."

Gary is still asleep but Jonny is up and about. He hears shuffling noise from Mandy's room. He knows she's up and about. His heart races with excitement knowing that he'll see her again soon. He's very much in love with her!

Mandy is up and ready to face the new day. She's feeling happy and energized and can hardly wait to see Jonny. She bravely and quietly steps out of her room. She tiptoes quietly trying not to disturb anyone that might be sleeping still. Jonny sees her while he's walking down from the top of the stairs. He's feeling playful. He watches her walk into the kitchen. He goes to the intercom panel in the hallway. He turns it on and uses the intercom for the kitchen.

He says, "Good Morning, Mandy! How are you today?" She had forgotten about their intercom system. She looks around the room a bit surprised.

She wasn't aware that he was up yet. They both laugh and she replies, "Jonny? You made my heart skip a beat. You're too funny! I'm fine and you? Are you coming downstairs now?"

He says, "Yes!" But this time he's standing at the threshold of the kitchen door and smiling at her. They both reach out and stand in a warm loving embrace sharing a few good morning kisses."

Gary says, "Good morning to both of you! How are you?" He's standing at the kitchen door, looking in and smiling.

Jonny says, "Good morning, Dad. How are you? I found an angel in our kitchen. It's a great way to start any day. Do you know when Sadie plans to cook for us this morning?"

"I just read a text message from her. She asked me to let her know when we're up and ready for breakfast. She said Charlie arrived and they're ready to join us. I replied with a text message a few minutes ago. I'm sure they'll walk through the door soon. I'll turn on the coffee pot. We can have a cup while we visit here until she arrives.

They hear the back door open and close as well as feet shuffling. They remove their shoes because they are wet from the snow on the ground. They enter the kitchen with big smiles and greet each other. Sadie says, "Good morning everyone. I'm planning to cook a big breakfast. It may be more like brunch by the time it's done. I've got eggs, sausage, hash browns, biscuits, toast and fresh fruit. Does that sound good? Is there anything you would like to add to the menu? Oh, I almost forgot. Charlie brought his favorite cinnamon rolls."

Mandy says, "WOW. That sounds like a delicious feast. I'm lucky to have tea and toast at home. What can I do to help you?"

Sadie replies, "Charlie offered to help me cook if that's okay? You can relax and enjoy your coffee."

Gary says, "That is a delicious feast, Mandy!" He chuckles. "I'm going to build a fire in the den's fireplace. We can relax with our coffee in there while Sadie and Charlie take over the kitchen." After he builds up the fire in the fireplace, he steps aside while he gives Katherine a call. He wants to surprise Mandy if her Mom decides to accept his invitation.

Katherine answers the phone with a cheerful greeting. She says, "Good morning Gary. How are you?"

Gary replies, "I'm doing fine. How are you? Would you like to surprise Mandy and join us for a brunch here at my house? Sadie and Charlie are just beginning to prepare the meal. If you would like to join us, I can drive out and pick you up."

"That sounds like fun, Gary. I drank a cup of coffee and ate a slice of toast. I'm not hungry now. It'll be great if you can pick me up. I'm nervous about driving on these roads. We have a lot of snow still blowing and drifting on the ground from the storm yesterday."

Gary says, "I can leave the house now if you're ready."

Katherine says, "Yes, I'll be ready to leave here when you arrive."

Gary says, "Thank you for accepting my invitation. I'll see you soon."

CHAPTER FIFTEEN
SUNDAY MORNING BRUNCH

Gary could sneak away to pick up Katherine but he tells Sadie and Charlie. He wants them to know about his plan to surprise Mandy. Also, they need to know there's one more guest to be seated at the table in the dining room.

Jonny and Mandy are drinking their coffee by the fireplace in the den. They're laughing and talking a lot. Jonny doesn't notice his Dad leaving the house.

The roads are clear and safe which made the trip to Katherine's house easier than anticipated. He walks up the sidewalk to her door and notices she's ready to leave the house. Gary wastes no time while driving Katherine to his house. He believes that Sadie and Charlie are close to serving the brunch.

When Gary and Katherine enter the house, they see and hear Jonny and Mandy setting the dining room table. Mandy looks up and is very surprised to see her Mom. She reacts with joy, "Oh, Mom! I'm so happy to see you and glad you're here in time for brunch. They are cooking a big delicious meal. Doesn't it smell good?" Mandy takes her Mom's jacket and accessories and hangs them up in the front closet for her. She gives her Mom a sweet and gentle hug and whispers "I love you, Mom?"

Her Mom replies, "I love you, too. The food smells delicious. I'm thankful Gary invited me to be here with you. I'm so happy to see you. What can I do to help?   Maybe I can help with the cleanup afterwards?!"

Gary says, "Please just relax Katherine. Let's go warm up by the fireplace in the den for a few minutes. Then we can come back for a cup of coffee. It appears that the brunch will be ready soon. I'm happy you're here."

Katherine replies, "I don't need to warm up by the fire. I'm fine. I'll wait here since we'll be sitting down at the table soon."

Gary asks, "Would you like a cup of coffee while you're waiting?"

"No, I can wait until we sit down. I had coffee at home earlier this morning."

Jonny and Mandy set the table in style. Sadie and Charlie serve the food in bowls and on trays. It's time for the family to gather around the table. It truly is a beautiful delicious feast. A real work of culinary art!

Sadie serves the coffee and offers refills. Once they're sitting comfortably, they give thanks each in their own special way. They take the time to relax and enjoy the company. They also enjoy the coffee and the delicious food Sadie and Charlie prepared for them. They made a great team in the kitchen. Lots of happy smiling faces are seen at this dining room table.   They're making new family memories.

Last year, there were only two family meals served in the dining room. Sadie's family along with the two Young men celebrated Thanksgiving and Christmas meals together.   The family count has grown with Charlie, Katherine and Mandy entering their lives this year. They consider this a wonderful reason to celebrate this holiday season. Their hearts are full of love both to give and receive. The Young Family liked to feel the Christmas Spirit all year long. They were very sad and lonely last year. But this year that feeling of sadness and loneliness has faded away.

After everyone is finished eating, Mandy, Katherine and Sadie get up and clear the table. The men can hear the ladies' laughter while they visit in the kitchen. The three ladies have the kitchen clean in a heartbeat.

The men sit and talk about a variety of topics while they sip the last of the coffee from their mugs. Gary asks Charlie, "How are your Aunt Polly and Uncle Pete doing? I've been thinking a lot about Thanksgiving Day plans. Do you think they would like to join us for a Thanksgiving meal? I enjoyed meeting them at their Pumpkin Patch."

Charlie replies, "They're doing fine now. The winter weather is hard on them. They have a good crew and the best farmhands anyone could hope for. Their commitment will see Aunt Polly and Uncle Pete through those hard winter months. Thank you for asking about them. I believe they'll appreciate your invitation for Thanksgiving Day. I'll be happy to check with them. but they traditionally travel to celebrate Thanksgiving with Aunt Polly's family."

Sadie walks in from the kitchen and asks Gary, "Have you invited Charlie and his Aunt and Uncle to join us for Thanksgiving Day yet?"

Gary says, "I just asked Charlie about inviting his aunt and uncle. He'll check with them but they might have previous plans. I didn't invite Charlie because I thought you might like to offer the Thanksgiving invitation. Are you ladies going to join us again?"

Sadie says, "Yes, we're refilling our coffee mugs and then we'll join you again at the table. This is a wonderful time for all of us to visit and chat about holiday plans."

Katherine sets her coffee mug at her place next to Gary. She asks him, "Would you like your coffee mug refilled?" He says, "Yes but I can refill it in a few minutes. Please try to relax. Thanks for the work you did in the kitchen!" She sits down in the chair next to him and tries to relax.

Mandy offers to refill Jonny's mug with coffee. He declines and says, "No thank you. Please try to relax, too. She sits next to Jonny again but this time they cuddle up."

Gary says, "I need to check on the fire in the fireplace. I'll be right back."

Katherine and Mandy have a chance to chat. Mandy shares her experiences in the mall yesterday. Charlie and Sadie step into the kitchen for a chat while Sadie refills his coffee mug. This is the time when Sadie wants to invite Charlie for Thanksgiving. She knows that Gary hasn't asked Katherine yet. She didn't want to spoil any special moments for him to ask her.

Sadie asks Charlie, "Would you do us the honor of joining us here on Thanksgiving Day? I'll roast a turkey with all the trimmings like I did last year. Gary plans to invite Katherine and Jonny will invite Mandy. My children and grandchildren are also invited. It'll be a blessing to have a big family celebration. You know much I love to cook big meals for Gary and Jonny. We believe the more the merrier." She giggles.

Charlie's eyes light up and he says, "I feel honored that you're inviting me. I feel blessed to be accepted and taken by this wonderful family. You can count me in. I'll be here on Thanksgiving Day for sure. If I can help in any way, please let me know."

They exchange a gentle hug and share the joy of the moment. They return to the dining table with their refilled coffee mugs. Their eyes meet and they smile at each other. They're thrilled with the thought of celebrating as one big happy family this year.

Sadie overhears Gary inviting Katherine. Evidently, Jonny invited Mandy and she accepted. Katherine replies, "I happily accept your invitation, Gary. It will be awesome sharing the day with Mandy here, too. I really do love this family and feel blessed to spend time with all of you. Thank you, Gary. Let me know if there's anything that I can do to help prepare the meal that day."

Mandy smiles at Jonny and says, "I'm so happy my Mom accepted your Dad's invitation." She dries tears of joy from her eyes. "Let me know, please, if I can do anything to help, too."

Gary speaks up and says, "The first thing we should do is talk about blending our family traditions. I want a fun-loving day for all of us. Sadie offered to roast the Turkey and prepare the trimmings. Let's figure out what trimmings we would like with the Turkey. I'm sure everyone has a favorite. We can make a special shopping list. The list doesn't have to be complete today. Planning ahead is a good idea."

Katherine says, "Perhaps it might help if we each brought our favorite dish to add to the meal. That could save Sadie some time and energy. I already plan on baking fresh pumpkin pies. I can bring those for our celebration."

Mandy says, "That sounds like a great idea. I can prepare my favorite dish if that's okay." I'll be glad to help in other ways too."

Gary says, "Sounds like we are off to a great start. I'm glad we took this time to share and plan the holiday ahead of time. Let's keep the lines of communication open. I believe this dining room table will be big enough for all of us including Sadie's children and grandchildren."

Sadie says, "We can also set up an extra table in this room if necessary. It's a big room. We can also add the center leaf to the table and add more chairs."

Gary says, "That's a good idea, Sadie. Fortunately, we don't have to make a final decision today. We can all move to the den for a chance to relax and enjoy the warmth of the fireplace."

Sadie says, "Thank you, Gary but Charlie and I have plans this afternoon. It would be best if we leave now. I need to go home to change clothes and freshen up. We'll say goodbye and hope to see you all again soon." They leave and walk over to Sadie's house.

Gary says, "Hope you both have a fun afternoon. There's still a lot of snow on the ground and it's cold. Stay warm and drive safe." He smiles at both in a caring way. "See you later! Thank you for cooking our delicious brunch. I thoroughly enjoyed our time together."

Jonny says, "Mandy and I want to play a few games in the basement. My muscles are still sore from yesterday. She wants to play pool. She'll probably beat me at every game we play. We'll see you later."

Gary asks Katherine, "Would you like to sit in the den with me by the fireplace? The warmth is comforting and I like relaxing by a roaring fire."

"Sure, but I have things to take care of at home. Will you give me a ride home soon, please?"

"I can drive you home at any time."

"I would like to relax by the fireplace with you, but I think it would be best to leave now. If that's okay, I'll say goodbye to Mandy."

"It's okay. I can use the intercom to call down to the basement. We can let Mandy know that you want to leave."

"That sounds good. I was hoping she would return upstairs so that we can say goodbye." Gary calls down to the basement, "Mandy? Your mom wants to leave for her house. Do you want to come upstairs and say goodbye?"

"I'll be right up." Mandy and Jonny leave the basement and rush up the stairs in a flash. Mandy and her Mom exchange hugs.

Mandy says, "Goodbye. I hope to see you again soon. I had a good time visiting with you, Mom. I hope you enjoyed the brunch. I'm glad you were here. Have a great week."

Her Mom says, "It was a great brunch and I'm happy to see you here. I hope to see you later and that you'll have a great week, too! I love you, Mandy!"

Mandy smiles and says, "I love you, Mom!"

Katherine turns and walks away toward the garage door. Gary escorts her to the car and helps her settle in to the passenger seat. He drives her home and walks with her up to the sidewalk." They exchange a gently hug and a soft kiss. She opens her door and walks in. She doesn't invite Gary in because she has things to do around her house. She feels the need to be alone.

He returns to his car. He thinks, *it's a good time for me to shop at the hardware store. I need to pick up more salt and deice pellets or maybe some sand. I'll stop there on my way home since I have this free time.*

Jonny calls his Dad on the cell phone. "Hi, Dad. How are you doing?"

His Dad replies, "Fine. I'm going to stop at the hardware store before I return home. How are you and Mandy doing? Can you please do me a favor and check on the fire? It was burning low when I left. It might be out by now."

"I'm going to drive Mandy back to her apartment in a few minutes. I'll make sure the fire is out before I leave. I'll see you later, Dad."

"Please tell Mandy goodbye for me. Let her know how much we appreciate her being a weekend family guest. She's a delight to be around and lights up the room."

"Thanks, Dad. I totally agree. She's a treasure and I enjoyed her stay with us, too." I'll tell her you said goodbye but I'm sure we'll all be together again soon. After all, Thanksgiving Day and related weekend festivities are right around the corner."

CHAPTER SIXTEEN
MAKING NEW FAMILY MEMORIES

The weather advisory on Halloween night was against spending time outdoors. They advised people should stay in for their safety. Lots of kids were disappointed that they could not go 'Trick-or-Treating in their neighborhood."

The pile of snow on the ground is bigger and it's getting colder. It's still autumn but the winter cold, ice and snow is moving in to the Omaha area. They dream of a white Christmas but not a white Halloween or Thanksgiving. Nonetheless, there's not a lot that anyone can do to change the weather. They'll make the best of it with neighbor helping neighbor.

It's Friday night, the second weekend in November, Jonny comes home from his office with a banker's box for his Dad. When his Dad opens it, he finds it filled with Thanksgiving Day cards and letters. They're from his friends. Most of the cards are from employees working in his businesses. Although he's overwhelmed with Joy, he's very surprised, too. Angela used to keep up with the holiday cards. She had a special gift in that area and sent out several lists of Christmas cards, too.

His Dad says, "Thanks for delivering these cards to me. Did you check to see if any of the cards are addressed to you personally? Maybe we can sit down and sort through the box. It'll take time to read through these cards and letters."

"I'm sure we can find time this weekend. I would like to sort through Mom's Thanksgiving decorations, tomorrow. Do you think we can do that together and set out her favorites? Thanksgiving is a couple of weeks away. Time sure flies by!"

His Dad replies, "I'm glad you mentioned the decorations. I would like to do that with you, Son. Your Mom is still with us in spirit. Between her decorations and these cards, it'll be a busy weekend for us."

Jonny says, "The temperature is going to be cold this weekend. Staying in and taking care of indoor projects is a good choice for us. I think Mandy would enjoy helping us with these projects. Would you be okay with that, Dad? Or would you prefer that it's just the two of us?"

His Dad answers, "Either way is fine with me. Mandy is welcome to join us. We need to make new holiday memories. She's so lovely and kind, I think she'll be very helpful."

"I'll send a text and ask if she's interested in joining us for a little decorating and sorting through the box of cards. I'll let you know when she replies. What do you want to eat for supper tonight, Dad?"

"Sadie is out with Charlie again tonight. We'll have to figure out a meal for ourselves. What would you like for supper, Jon?"

Jonny replies, "I don't really know yet. I'll have to give it a little more thought. Let me know what you decide." Jonny sends a text to Mandy inviting her over to help them with their projects." She's excited about the chance to decorate with Angela's treasures. Mandy asks, "Have you made supper plans? I can cook a meal for you here at my apartment for a change. Your Dad is welcome to join us, too. I have sirloin steak and baked potatoes on my mind. I can make salads for you two, also. I'll heat up the apple cider."

"Sounds great, Mandy, but let me check with my Dad. I don't think he's seen your apartment. It'll be a great change of pace for us." He tells his Dad about Mandy's dinner invitation. Gary is grateful for the invitation and accepts with a big smile.

Jonny calls her instead of a text to let her know that they're on the way. He also asks, "Is there anything we can bring or do to help your meal preparation." She replies "No, I have everything I need right here. Drive safe, I'll see you soon."

It's freezing outside but thank goodness, the roads are well maintained. Jonny drives since he knows the way there. They arrive at Mandy's apartment without any problems. Mandy hears their car and opens the door for them to walk right in. The aroma of hot spiced apple cider fills the air.

Mandy says, "Would you like a cup of hot cider to help you warm up after that cold trip over here?"

"Sounds great, Mandy dear. I really like your apartment. It has a warm caring atmosphere. You and Jonny did a great job decorating for the Thanksgiving holiday. The harvest decorations are lovely both inside and outside."

Jonny says, "I can serve the apple cider to you and Dad." He goes to her kitchen cabinet and serves the apple cider in her fancy holiday mugs. Gary and Jonny sit at her kitchen table while they drink the cider and chat with her.

Jonny offers to prepare the salad. Gary declines the offer for a salad but he offers to help make it. The men prepare the salad while Mandy bakes the potatoes in the oven.

She asks, "Gary, would you prefer a different vegetable? I might be able find something you like in the freezer. How do you like your steak cooked?"

Gary replies, "I prefer medium well." Jonny nods in agreement that he would like the same. "No need to cook an extra side for me. I'll be fine with the steak and potato."

She says, "Good choice. That's how I like my steak, too. I don't cook as well as Sadie or the chefs at 'Ted's Steakhouse'. My Mom taught me how to cook but I don't have a lot of experience. Just like Sadie, I enjoy cooking and baking."

The salad is ready and in chilling in the refrigerator. Jonny offers to set the table. Mandy says, "That's okay. I'll do that. Try to relax. The food will be ready to eat in a few more minutes."

She cooks the steak to perfection on a stovetop griddle. The timer dings on the oven letting her know that the potatoes are done. She removes the baked potatoes and quickly sets the table for the three of them. In a flash, she sets out the butter and sour cream, the salad with dressing and the salt and pepper shakers.

She announces, "The meal is ready to eat. Would you like a beverage with your meal? They indicate that the cider is fine.

The three of them sit down at the kitchen table and enjoy their meal while they visit. It's delicious! Jonny and Gary are both impressed and grateful. They're very satisfied!"

Mandy says, "I'm sorry that I don't have a dessert to offer you."

Jonny says, "That's okay. I'm too full for dessert right now." Gary nods in agreement with Jonny.

Mandy inquires, "What time do you want to decorate? I'm totally free tomorrow. I can drive over tomorrow around early afternoon. That should give us enough time to sort through the box of cards. Does that work for you?"

Jonny says, "That's perfect, Mandy! I look forward to working on the projects with you at home tomorrow." He stands up and clears the table. He rinses the dishes and stacks them in the sink. "Would you like another mug of cider? There's more here in the pan."

Mandy's says, "No, I'm good." Gary also passes on his offer. There's not a lot to do in Mandy's apartment. They decide to sit in the living room. She has a couch and stuffed chair. Gary chooses to relax in the chair while Mandy and Jonny cuddle up on the couch. Gary and Jonny do not watch TV at home. Mandy has a nice TV set up in the room. She offers them a chance to watch TV or a holiday movie. They both decline her offer. Gary and Jonny are outdoor type people. They feel a bit bored now that the weather is cold and they're stuck indoors.

She asks for suggestions. "What would you like to do this evening?"

Jonny replies. "What do you normally do?"

"When I'm home alone, I like to watch TV, movies and sometimes I read before bed. I try to rest and relax as often as I can after a long work week. I admit that I don't have guests in my home very often. Mom doesn't visit with me here very often either."

His Dad says, "Jonny maybe we should leave so that she can relax and rest up for tomorrow. Tomorrow will be a busy day. We'll all need energy to complete these projects."

Jonny says, "It's getting late. We'll go now, Mandy! Thank you for your hospitality and a delicious meal. I'll drive out and pick you up tomorrow early afternoon." He gives her a sweet and gentle hug goodbye and a kiss on her check while standing at the front door.

Mandy gives Gary a friendly goodbye hug before he walks out the door. Gary says, "Good night, Mandy dear. Thank you for a wonderful time. I enjoyed it very much! We'll see you tomorrow."

Gary and Jonny leave and drive home. Mandy loads the dishes in the dishwasher. She changes into her comfy pajamas and bathrobe. She's tired but feeling the joy of the evening she spent with Jonny and his Dad. She cuddles under a fleece throw on her couch. When she turns on the TV, she finds a holiday movie. She lays her head back, sighs and relaxes there until bed time.

When Jonny and Gary arrive home to an empty house, they feel lonely. There's been a lot of family activity there recently. Now it's too quiet. Gary decides to brew a pot of fresh coffee. There's leftover cobbler in the refrigerator. He builds a fire in the fireplace in the den.

He asks, "Son, would you like to sit me in the den by the fireplace. We can relax a bit there while we eat a slice of cobbler and drink a cup of coffee."

"I like relaxing by the fire when it's cold outside. The cobbler and coffee sounds like a great treat after Mandy's delicious meal. I'm tired from a busy workweek so I'll be ready to call it a night soon. Just relax, Dad. I'll serve the cobbler and coffee for us in the den."

Jonny goes to the kitchen while his Dad settles in his favorite place in the den. Jonny pours coffee in the mugs and sets them on a serving tray. Two slices of pie are served on two saucers. He carries the tray into the den and sets it on the table next to his Dad. Jonny places his mug and saucer on a table next to a chair that he'll sit on. The crackling sound of the fire warms Gary's heart. They both try to relax but it's difficult because their minds are working overtime. They relive a lot of memories from the past as well as the new ones from this year.

Jonny places the empty mugs and saucers back on the serving tray and carries it back to the kitchen. He rinses the dishes and adds them to the dishwasher.

He returns to check on his Dad in the den. He says, "Dad, are you doing okay? I would like to take time to call Mandy before I go to sleep tonight. Are you going to be okay, if I go upstairs now? Do you want me to do anything for you?"

"No, I'm going to stay and watch the fire a little longer. I find it to be very warm and relaxing. I'll go upstairs soon. Enjoy your chat with Mandy! I'll see you in the morning. Good night! I love you, Son.

"I love you, too, Dad. See you in the morning. Good night."

Jonny is worried about his Dad. He knows how hard it is on him to be stuck indoors over the cold winter months. He thinks, *Maybe I can convince Dad to schedule a holiday cruise. He still has a dream to travel. I'll try to remember to talk to him about it this weekend.*

Jonny walks upstairs to his bedroom. He changes into night clothes and freshens up. His cell phone rings and is surprised that Mandy is calling him. Perfect! He snuggles up in the comforter in his bed while he talks with Mandy. She's also snuggled up in her bed.

She's calling to say, "Thanks again for your visit in my apartment. It was a lot of fun for me."

He assures her, "It was our pleasure. We'll see you tomorrow. Sleep well."

"I'm about to fall asleep now, I'm very relaxed and happy thanks to you, Jonny. Good night, I love you!"

"I love you. Good night."

CHAPTER SEVENTEEN
GIVING THANKS

Mandy has been up for several hours. She'll be ready to go, when Jonny picks her up around noon. She's excited about their plan to work on two family projects with his Dad. When Jonny arrives, he's excited about picking up Mandy and returning home. They took time to greet each other with their usual hello hugs and kisses.

Jonny asks, "Thank you for your willingness to help us out. Would it be okay if you brought your laptop? Dad and I would like for you to prepare a spreadsheet for us. We think from our experience, that is the most convenient way to organize names and addresses. You can copy them from the Thanksgiving cards' and letters' envelopes. If you prefer to use our computers at home, that is okay, too. Using your laptop will be easier on you. We can get the job done faster."

"I don't mind at all. I look forward to getting the job done as quickly as possible. I know it means a lot to your Dad. I'm happy to help in any way possible."

When they arrive at his Dad's house, they immediately feel a warm wonderful atmosphere. The fire is crackling in the fireplace and the flames are daintily dancing. The glow of the fire casts shadowy images on the wall, ceiling and floor.

His Dad is sitting in the den relaxing by the fireplace. He stands and welcomes Mandy with a gentle hug. He says, "I'm so grateful that you're here and will add your feminine touch to our family projects today."

"I'm happy to be here. I think it will be fun to work on these projects with you two. I realize that I'll never replace Angela but I'm happy to try to follow in her footsteps. The power of the love you two shared is very strong. Her energy lingers here in a beautiful way."

Jonny asks, "Dad, which project would you like to start first? Do we want to decorate for Thanksgiving or organize the Thanksgiving cards and letters?"

His Dad asks, "Mandy, which project would you like to work on first?"

She replies, "I'm excited to see Angela's treasured Thanksgiving items. Is it okay if we work on that project first?"

Jonny replies, "I've already carried the storage box from the basement. We can work at the dining room table. We can unpack the decorations safely there. Last year, Sadie helped us with the decorating but she has plans with Charlie."

They walk from the den to the dining room. She sits on a chair to watch them unpack the box. She thinks, *I know how special these memories are for them. I'm glad to be here in the moment but I also feel the need to give them space.*

They share stories with her about the special memories attached to her favorite decorations. She's all eyes and ears while she watches and listens to them share.

Mandy says, "There's a lot of beautiful items that I've never seen before any place else."

Gary shares with Mandy, "Several of these items are antiques. Angela inherited them from her parents and grandparents. Angela purchased a few around town but they were all meaningful to her. We treasure these items because her memory is attached. When I see these items, it's easy to recall the memory of her smile and laughter. She loved to give to others by giving of herself and was quick to give thanks. She enjoyed planning our family Thanksgiving weekend celebrations. She was a wonderful blessing to all of us."

Mandy shares with Jonny and his Dad, "I really adore the cornucopia. It's very colorful and festive. Where do you usually display it?"

Jonny laughs and shares, "Dad and I crafted it for my Mom when I was fourteen years old. She loved it because we created it for her." He pauses and asks his Dad, "Do you remember helping me make this decoration for Mom?"

"I sure do, Jon. I remember how happy she was to receive it. She definitely counted it as her favorite treasure above and beyond these valuable antiques."

Jonny replies to Mandy, "We usually place this in the center of the dining room table. It's our centerpiece when we serve our Thanksgiving meal." He pauses again for a minute as though he's reliving the memory. "Would you like to continue the tradition this year?"

"Yes, Son. It's a beautiful reminder. Although she's not with us physically, I believe, she's still with us in spirit. I also believe, our loved ones that have gone before us are smiling down from above. Our memories of them are kept alive by the power of our undying love."

"You know that I agree with you, Dad. They exchange a quick comforting hug. Mandy gives them a comforting hug, while saying, "I believe in what you just shared. I feel that way about my Dad. I believe his spirit is with my Mom and I, too."

Jonny asks, "Now that the box is unpacked and all the decorations are on the table, shall we decide the best place for them?"

His Dad says, "If I recall correctly, these two antiques were display on a shelf in the curio cabinet located in the den." Mandy, would you like to find a place on the shelf for these two items?"

"Sure. Jonny, I know this is a special time for you, would you like to do this together? We'll be sharing a new family memory." They smile lovingly and in the most understanding way.

Gary chooses a couple of items that will look great on the fireplace mantel. The first one is a ceramic figurine. It's a little cherub inside a wreath made with autumn leaves. The banner reads, "Give Thanks.: The second one is like the first figurine but has a banner with the words "Happy Thanksgiving". He believes he made a great choice because he placed them on either side of a frame that holds Angela's photo. While admiring her beauty, he remembers the love they shared. He thinks, *Happy Thanksgiving, Angela. I still love and miss you!"*

Jonny and Mandy return to the dining room table. They wait for his Dad to return from the den. Jonny asks, "What do you want us to do, now? I guess Sadie spoiled me by knowing just what to do. She's a talented lady. It's too bad that she couldn't be with us today. I'm happy she is out and about with Charlie. They seem to have a good time together."

He smiles at Mandy and says, "I'm very happy you're here with us today." She smiles and they hug each other lovingly. "I'm happy to make new Thanksgiving memories with you and Dad."

His Dad replies, "I agree, Jonny and Mandy, the time we're sharing today is quality and precious memories. Which one of you would like to hang this autumn wreath on the front door?" I've got a hanger here that you can place at the top of the door. The hook drops down low enough for you to the hang the wreath."

Mandy asks, "Jonny, why don't we hang this wreath together? I'm not quite tall enough to place the hanger at the top of the door." Jonny agrees. They take off for the front door. He takes advantage of the few minutes that they are alone to steal several kisses along with a warm embrace and warm smiles. After properly hanging the wreath, they return to the dining table. His Dad is looking a little pale and is now sitting on a chair.

Jonny asks, "Dad? Are you okay?"

His Dad replies, "Yes, but I missed lunch. It's late afternoon. I probably should take a break and eat lunch now. There are only few more items here. We can finish up quick then we can all eat lunch. Would you like to place these figurines on the coffee table in the living room? Maybe we can hang this "Give Thanks" plaque on a wall in the kitchen. Here's a Thanksgiving trivet that can go into the kitchen also."

"I've got it Dad. I'll hang the plaque after lunch."

His Dad says. "Let's see. "Would it be okay if we repackage the rest in the storage box. I believe we have enough of her decorations for now. There will be a lot more people in this house this Thanksgiving. I don't want to over decorate and feel crowded."

"Yes, I agree with you, Dad. It's a good idea to keep the rest in storage for safekeeping. I'll wrap the items that are left and carry the box back down to the storage closet in the basement."

After he secures the box of his Mom's decorations, he returns from the basement. He asks, "What would you like to eat for lunch, Dad? Please come and relax at the kitchen table, while I prepare our lunch. We can chat about our next project."

His Dad sits at the kitchen table and tries to relax. He requests soup and sandwich for lunch. Mandy helps Jonny prepare soup and sandwiches for three. His Dad says there's not a lot we can chat about regarding the box of cards and letters. We can play it by ear and figure out what's what when the time comes."

Mandy says, "I brought my laptop with software to make a spreadsheet listing names and addresses. We can add more columns as you need them. I know how much the holiday and the cards mean to both of you. I'll help as much as I can."

After they finish eating, Gary is feeling reenergized. He's grateful for Mandy's talent in organizing this project for them. The work together at the dining room table. She sets up her laptop and creates a new spreadsheet titled 'Thanksgiving 2016'. Jonny lifts the lid on the banker's box. They sort Thanksgiving cards from the letter size envelopes. They decided to open all the cards first. Jonny uses a letter opener to tear the top of the envelopes. After

Jonny and his Dad read each card, they pass it on to Mandy. She copies the name and address (if there is one) into the spreadsheet. Some of the cards are only addressed with a handwritten name. Most are for Gary from employees that are his friends. There's a card from Ted Harris and his family. That brings a smile to his face. There are several addressed to Jonny from employees and friends. People dropped off several cards at the office for convenience sake. A few of the cards are addressed to Gary and Jonny. They feel blessed to have so many friends and business acquaintances.

Mandy has a long list of names in the first column. In the second column is a list of their addresses. In the third column, she has 'card' or 'letter' marked next to the name. They will take a little extra care in replying to the letters. Jonny and his Dad look over Mandy's shoulder for a quick look at the screen. They're more than pleased at the great job she did for them. It's very organized and saved them a lot of time and trouble.

Gary asks, "Can you please copy that file on this external hard drive? I can open that file on my computer and print off address labels as I need them. I'll probably spend time tomorrow addressing cards and letters in reply to those we have received. I'm not sure if I have enough cards for all these people. I'll go out to the store in a few minutes to buy a couple of boxes. Thank you for your awesome assistance."

Mandy says, "Done! It only takes a minute to copy that file for you. You're welcome. I enjoy working on computer projects. It was my pleasure to assist you.

Jonny says, "I'll stop at the store for you, Dad, when I take Mandy home. I'll buy several boxes of Thanksgiving cards for variety. Mandy and I need a few for our family and friends, too. If you want our help, we'll be here for you tomorrow."

"Sounds great, Son. Thanks! Thanksgiving will be here before we realize it. Time sure flies."

Jonny shares with his Dad, "Mandy and I were chatting earlier about Thanksgiving Day. She suggested that she could make a couple of lists on her laptop. One list for projected menu that also lists favorite dishes that people are bringing to the table. For example, Katherine plans to bring fresh baked pumpkin pie and whipped cream. Charlie has a favorite candied yam dish that he wants to bring. Another list can show the confirmed number of people who will eat the meal with us on Thanksgiving Day. I know the people we invited plan to show up but I'm not sure about Sadie's family yet."

Mandy says, "I can start a running shopping list for the items we need to complete the menu. It might be helpful to Sadie, if we add items to the shopping list today."

Gary says, "That sounds great you two. Thanks so much for your help in finalizing our family plans to celebrate this special holiday. I'm hoping for a peaceful, loving and joyful Thanksgiving Day.

CHAPTER EIGHTEEN
HAPPY THANKSGIVING

It's the third weekend in November. Thanksgiving is Thursday which is only a few days away.

Sadie plans to shop at the local grocery store and market today. Mandy assists Sadie by completing and printing the shopping list of food items for the holiday meal. Sadie invites Katherine and Mandy to shop with her. Sadie enjoys their company and thinks they might enjoy the outing. The stores are decorated for the holidays. Katherine and Mandy accepts her offer and they have a fun time getting the job done together.

One of the items on the list is fresh cranberries. Gary wants to make fresh cranberry sauce using one of Angela's favorite recipes.

Jonny likes the spinach salad that his Grandma prepared for a holiday meal several years ago. He asked Sadie to buy the ingredients for him to cook it on Thursday.

After the shopping trip is complete, Katherine and Mandy decide to spend the rest of the day together. They want to do a little pre-Christmas shopping. There are several sales at the mall. It's a fun time for the two of them.

Sadie sits down with Jonny and his Dad at the kitchen table while they drink a mug of hot apple cider. She goes over the final lists and menu with him.

She says, "My children told me today that they will not be joining us for the Thanksgiving meal. They spent the holiday with us last year. This year their spouses are expecting them to spend the holiday with their in-laws. They would like to bring the grandkids over later in the day for a visit. We can plan on them joining us in time for dessert. Katherine and I plan to bake fresh pumpkin pies. That should be enough pie for the whole family to enjoy."

Gary says, "I'm sorry to hear that your children and grandchildren will not be able to join us for the feast. I certainly understand why they would want to share the holidays with extended family. It'll be great if they make it in time to visit over pie and coffee. I look forward to seeing them. You have a great family. Your grandchildren are the best."

"Thanks, Gary! Now, here's what the menu looks like. I'll roast the turkey with stuffing. If you agree with my suggestions, I'll prepare mashed potatoes, gravy, corn and dinner rolls for our Thanksgiving Day feast. Charlie plans to prepare candied yams at his house and bring the dish over that day. Jonny said he wants to cook spinach salad. The final food item is your homemade cranberry sauce. Oh, yes, I bought eggnog and more apple cider for beverages to add to our meal. Can you think of anything that's not on the list?"

Jonny replies, "What about Mandy's dish? She wants to add a favorite dish to the meal, too. Let's see if I can remember?! Oh, yes, it's a vegetable dish made with steamed broccoli and cauliflower with cheese. Sounds delicious, doesn't it?" He smiles.

Sadie says, "Yes it does. I'll add that to the menu right now. I think it's finally complete unless you two think of something else between now and then."

The days pass quickly. Thanksgiving Day has arrived! There's a lot of early morning hustle and bustle in the Young family household. Sadie prepares breakfast for the two Young men just as she always does. After the kitchen is clean again, she goes to work prepping the turkey. She stuffs it with dressing and places it in a roasting pan. She preheats the oven and places the roasting pan inside.

While the turkey is roasting in the oven, Gary boils the fresh cranberries in a pan on the stovetop. When they boil down, he'll follow Angela's recipe to complete the cranberry sauce for the meal.

Jonny's spinach salad is easy to prepare so he plans to wait until his Dad is cooking in the kitchen. He's on the phone with Mandy now. "Do you want to drive over in your car or would you like for me to drive out and pick you up?"

Mandy says, "I would prefer that you drive because the weather forecast says more snow is on the way today. It's going to be a white Thanksgiving."

"Oh, Mandy, I did not listen to the forecast this morning. I didn't know. I'm glad you told me. I better let my Dad know. I hope everyone has safe travels on the snow-covered roads."

Mandy says, "I'm thankful that they're not predicting a blizzard. It's supposed to be a light snow. I would still prefer that you drive because I don't like driving at night especially with snow on the streets."

"Yes, I'm glad it's not a blizzard, too. I'll be happy to drive over and pick you up as well as drive you home tonight.   What time do you want to be here?"

"I'm ready for you to pick me up at any time. I'm looking forward to spending our first Thanksgiving Day with you and your family. I'm also happy that my Mom will be there. Has she arrived at your house yet?"

"No, your Mom is not here yet. I should let you go.   I want to tell my Dad about the snow in the forecast. He might want to offer your Mom a ride, too. I'll see you soon."

"Okay, the front door will be unlocked for you."

Jonny finds his Dad in the kitchen working on the cranberry sauce. He tells him, "Mandy just told me about the weather forecast. More snow is on the way today. I'm going to drive over and pick her up. I thought you might want to know. Is there a chance that Katherine will need a ride, too? Mandy and I can swing by her place and give her a ride."

His Dad replies, "I'll give her call myself and offer her a ride.   The cranberry sauce is just about ready to chill in the refrigerator. Thanks, Jon!"

"I'll cook my spinach salad when I return. It's an easy dish to prepare. I'll see you later, Dad."

In the meantime, Sadie has basted the turkey at least twice. Charlie is on his way with his favorite candied yams. Sadie baked the pumpkin pies at her house last night. They are chilling in her refrigerator for later in the day. She also whipped fresh cream to top each slice of pie. Now that Gary is out of the kitchen, she peels the potatoes and puts them in a pot to boil on the stovetop.

The dinner rolls are frozen. She removes the package from the freezer. Per the directions, she places the individual rolls in the muffin pan to defrost. As soon as the turkey is removed from the oven, the rolls will go in to bake.

Gary calls Katherine and she accepts his offer for a ride. She's thankful that she won't have to drive home when it's dark and snowing. While he's out picking her up, Charlie arrives at the house with a dish of candied yams that he prepared. Sadie sets it on the counter on a warming tray and keeps the dish covered. Jonny arrives shortly after with Mandy and her vegetable dish. There's room on the warming tray to keep her broccoli and cauliflower with cheese warm until it's ready to be served on the table.

Everything is falling in place in a well-organized way. Jonny cooks his spinach salad while Sadie mashes the potatoes and makes gravy. He's done in a flash and adds his dish to the warming tray. Jonny, Mandy, and Charlie ask Sadie about the place settings at the table. Mandy says, "I can make place cards really quick."

Sadie replies, "Gary should sit at the head of the table. Katherine and Mandy can be seated on the left-hand side of the table. Jonny at the other end of the table with Charlie and I on the right-hand side of the table. How does that sound?"

Mandy says, "Perfect! I don't think we'll need place cards." She laughs.

With Sadie's instructions and guidance, Charlie, Mandy and Jonny set the table beautifully. They used a Thanksgiving theme tablecloth and napkins. Sadie gives them the special holiday plates from a kitchen cabinet. She also provides fancy mugs for the cider and holiday glasses for the eggnog. Angela's cornucopia centerpiece is perfectly placed on the table.

Gary arrives with Katherine after a short delay. The snow fall made a few side streets impassible. They're both thankful that the road conditions were good enough to arrive home safely. Katherine stores her pumpkin pies with the whipped topping in the refrigerator for later in the day.

They look at the table with awe. It's truly beautiful! The atmosphere in the whole house is warm and inviting. Gary decides to make a fire in the fireplace. They'll be free to relax in the den by the fireplace.

Jonny's Dad asks, "Son, do you think you're up to shoveling the sidewalk and sprinkling it with sand? Let's celebrate the holiday with our family meal. Sadie's kids and grandkids will join us later for pumpkin pie. I want them to be safe on the sidewalk."

"Yes, Mandy and I can get the job done together." He laughs. "It'll give us another chance to have a snowball fight. I should bring my camera out this time and take pictures of her throwing snowballs at me." They both laugh. "I'm going to get my camera now and start taking family photos. I'll want a picture of the table set up so beautifully with Mon's cornucopia."

Gary says, "You might find a photo moment in the den, too!"

Jonny takes a few random photos and sets the camera down close to the dining room table. Sadie finds Gary and says, "The turkey is done and ready to carve. Do you want to carve it in the kitchen or at the table? I have the serving tray in the kitchen."

"I'll carve it in the kitchen. Hopefully it'll be less messy in there." He smiles. He walks into the kitchen and the aroma of fresh rolls is intoxicating. While he's carving the turkey, Sadie is setting the serving bowls on the dining room table. Everything is cooked and ready to eat.

She offers to serve beverages. They unanimously reply, "You've already done more than your share of work here. We can get our own beverage. It's time for you to sit down and relax. Charlie pulls out a chair for her to sit down. He sits down next to her. Gary pulls out Katherine's chair and they take their place at the table. Jonny pulls out the chair for Mandy but before he sits down he reaches over for his camera and takes a family photo.

This day is very special to the Young family. Jonny and Mandy are thankful to share their first Thanksgiving Day here at the Young family home. His Dad uses the camera to take another photo of the family sitting around the table. He doesn't want Jon to be left out of the Young family album. He knows that a photo with Mandy will be a treasured Thanksgiving memory in years to come. He also focuses the camera on Charlie and Sadie as a couple. He hands the camera back to Jon. Jon snaps another photo of his Dad seated beside Katherine.

Just as Gary had hoped for, this Thanksgiving Day family celebration turned out to be loving, peaceful and joyful. He feels thankful for a long list of things. Gary says, "I'm thankful that you could join us on this special family holiday. Relax and enjoy this delicious meal. A big 'Thank You' to all of you for cooking and sharing your favorite holiday dishes. Happy Thanksgiving Day to everyone!"

Everyone but Jonny says, "Happy Thanksgiving, Gary. Thank you for inviting us." Jonny follows by saying, "Happy Thanksgiving, Dad!"

Gary places a slice of turkey on his plate and passes the tray next to Katherine. Each one fills their plate with the delicious food. They 'give thanks' in their own special way.

Jonny and Mandy finish eating first. He says, "Excuse me, for a few minutes, I see the snow is falling in huge snowflakes. We need to clear the sidewalk for Sadie's family. They should be arriving any time now."

Jonny and Mandy go to the garage. Jonny grabs the snow shovel and Mandy picks up the container of sand for the sidewalk. They work together to clear the sidewalk

As if on cue, Mandy throws the first snowball. The snowball fight doesn't last long. Sadie's two children drive up to the curb. They're thankful that the sidewalk was cleared for them. The little grandchildren are excited to see Mandy and Jonny again. They exchange hugs and smiles with a Happy Thanksgiving greeting.

They make their way down the sidewalk safely and into the house. Jonny and Mandy leave the shovel leaning against the side of the house and the sand by the porch. They know that they'll need to use it again before Sadie's children leave to return home.

They go inside and hear happy chatter and laughter. Everyone is thankful to be together as one big happy family on Thanksgiving Day.

They set up an extra table and chairs in the dining room. It's time for the pumpkin pie with whipped cream topping. The grandchildren are thrilled that Nana baked pumpkin pie.

Gary and Mandy choose to eat a slice of Katherine's pumpkin pie. Both pies are delicious and basically the same recipe.

Jonny stands by his Dad's chair. He says, "Thank you so much, Dad, for this wonderful day. I'm so thankful to be a part of a big happy family. We made a lot of wonderful new family memories while celebrating Thanksgiving today. Like Mom always said, "It's a holiday for Giving Thanks!"

EPILOGUE

Jonny and his Dad are thankful for many autumn blessings. Thanksgiving turned out to be a happy family day. It was a celebration filled with love, peace and joy. On the following Saturday, they decide to follow Angela's longtime habit. They gather together the autumn decorations from inside and outside of the house just like she used to do. Jonny and his Dad work together outside to remove the pumpkins along with other autumn items. There's at least a foot of snow which made it difficult to do the job. Mandy helped with the work inside the house

They wrap and store Angela's favorite autumn treasures in the same box that she stored them in. Jonny carries it down to the closet in the basement for safekeeping. Traditionally, she would locate the boxes in the same storage closet marked 'Christmas'. She would carry those boxes upstairs to the dining room table. With great joy, she would ask Jonny and Gary to help her sort the decorations. They helped her decorate both inside and outside. Christmas was the Young family's favorite holiday.

Today, while Jonny was storing his Mom's box of autumn decorations, he also located the boxes marked 'Christmas'. He carried them upstairs to the dining room table. This time, he'll ask his Dad and his bride-to-be, Mandy, to help him sort the decorations. This weekend, they plan to decorate the inside and the outside of their house for Christmas. Christmas time is still the Young family's favorite time of the year.

ABOUT THE AUTHOR

I'm a wife, Mom of 3, Mom-in-law, Gramma to 7, sister, aunt, with cousins by the dozens. I love spending quality time with my family, friends & extended family. We currently reside in Nebraska.

My pen name, Lola, was created by merging the first two letters (LO) of my name with the first two letters (LA) of my husband's name. He is my proofreader, encouragement and support.

I've always loved WORDS! I appreciate puns, word games & creative writing. I've enjoyed writing original music with Christian lyrics, Christian poems and other poems in the past. This year, I felt overwhelmed with passion to write my first novel, 'Love Grows in Omaha'. I have hopes of writing sequels about the Young Family. My favorite stories are about love, family and commitment. I enjoy watching movies and reading books that are romantic comedies.

My hobbies/interests include creating fun videos while singing Karaoke as a member of an online community, camping in our RV, picnics by the lake, baking, photography, creating art, listening to relaxation music and lots more. These hobbies help me cope with multiple health challenges daily. I'm also hearing and vision impaired.

My favorite flowers are pink sweetheart roses. I wish you all love, peace and joy!

Love Always,

Lola aka Lois